A VILLAGE CALLED CHRISTMAS

Jodie Homer

To
Jean

from
Jodie

CONTENTS

Title Page

Copyright

Acknowledgement

Summary

Other books by the author

Chapter 1	1
Chapter 2	6
Chapter 3	11
Chapter 4	18
Chapter 5	24
Chapter 6	31
Chapter 7	39
Chapter 8	49
Chapter 9	56
Chapter 10	62
Chapter 11	72
Chapter 12	83

Chapter 13	94
Chapter 14	102
Chapter 15	108
Chapter 16	121
Chapter 17	129
Chapter 18	137
Chapter 19	144
Chapter 20	155
Chapter 21	167
Chapter 22	177
Chapter 23	187
Chapter 24	191
Chapter 25	195
Chapter 26	206
Thank you	214
Trademark Acknowledgement	217
About The Author	221
Social Media	223
Meet You In the Summer	225

ACKNOWLEDGEMENT

Here we are again and this time I have many people to thank for helping me with this book. First of all my family who support and love me. My husband especially who makes all my covers. I love how special they are and I appreciate how much time and effort it takes to make them look good. I also want to thank my lovely friend and editor Becky who puts up with my nagging as well as my million spelling mistakes and grammar issues. I promise I'm getting better at it now. I want to thank my friends from Chicklit and Prosecco who answer my annoying questions and issues and who continue to support and chat daily to me about everything. So thank you Jaimie Admans, Bettina Hunt, Leonie Mack, Kitty Wilson and Bernadette Maycock. Lastly, I want to thank everyone who betas for me and who continues to communicate through social media with me. I love our little community.

SUMMARY

Is the answer to Holly's broken heart hidden in a village called Christmas?

Holly loves Christmas but when she comes home and catches her boyfriend in bed with her boss she escapes her life and ends up in a village called Christmas. When she meets the Claus family she begins to realise it definitely does take a community to celebrate Christmas. As she gets stuck into the village festivities can the dashing single farmer Joseph Claus fix her heartbreak? Is the answer to Holly's broken heart hidden in a village called Christmas?

OTHER BOOKS BY THE AUTHOR

Raindrops on the Umbrella Café
A Magical Christmas on the Isle of Skye
Married By Thirty

CHAPTER 1

I absolutely love Christmas. I know loads of people say that but I do. I work in a Christmas shop called Deck the Aisles. Today is the first day we are allowed to wear our Christmas jumpers to work. It's not yet December but it already feels festive. The sky is full of grey and white clouds and the fog is clouding my view. I'm already wearing my Christmas jumper and Santa hat. Corporate says we can from the first of November but most people don't until December. My manager Kelly says I'm like the Christmas spirit and I guess I am. I just love Christmas.

I also love Christmas jumpers which we sell lots of and I really enjoy looking through all of the sparkly ones. I have loved designing clothes since I was little and my mum used to help me make clothes for my Barbies.

I walk into work as Nat King Cole blasts through the speakers overhead and I hum along as I put my coat and hat away.

Today, I'm really excited about decorating the store tree. While I watch from the window the children line up with their parents on the first day the grotto is open.

"There you are and already in a Christmas jumper," My best friend and co-worker Carol says. It's rather ironic that we are so close and she doesn't care about Christmas.

"Of course," I say, and whistle the last line of 'A Christmas Song'. She rolls her eyes at me.

"You're way too happy this morning," she says, wearing our uniform of black trousers and a smart red button-up shirt.

"Of course I am, it's nearly December," I say, enthusiastically.

"Oh no, it's that time of the year again." Jake comes in dressed in his uniform looking like he has just rolled out of bed.

Kelly storms in with a hard look on her face and walks straight over to us.

"Jake, go and switch the sample Santa Clauses on for customers, Carol you are on snack sampling today and Holly you will be teaching the newbies the basics."

Carol rolls her eyes. That means she'll be spending most of her shift handing out party snacks and mince pies but not being able to eat a single one herself.

I wait with a smile on my face for the gaggle of newbies that come piling out of the backroom. Late, of course, but it doesn't matter. It's only nine am and we don't usually get many shoppers first thing. Kelly wants a couple of them to help her and I'll be training the lucky ones on gift wrapping. I always add bows to make it special.

I round the ones up that are in our department and begin to show them the basic check-out skills they need and how to wrap presents. My morning flies by and it's eleven am before I know it. I take off my Santa hat and swap places with one of the newbie singers. At the front of the store there is always one of us dressed as an elf singing Christmas tunes, with a bucket to collect for charity.

I start with Jingle Bells, singing really enthusiastically, whilst wishing our shoppers a Merry Christmas and before going for a bit of Mariah? (because who doesn't love Mariah)

Jake brings me a gingerbread latte from the café at the back of the store.

"Thanks, you're an angel," I say sitting back in my chair, exhausted.

"You can thank me later." Jake winks and I slap him.

"Did you see Luke?" I ask. My boyfriend Luke has been helping out at the café over the holiday season. He is actually an environmental inspector but he told me he has the holidays off so he needed a Christmas job

"Mhm," he says noncommittally "Well," I ask impatiently.

"Well?" Jake starts. "He's the same wanker he always is."

I give him the eye.

"He's right," Carol says.

I sigh. I wish my friends weren't like this with Luke. I know I'm fussy and I can't keep a boyfriend usually past a year but this Christmas Eve will be exactly a year for us.

"No, he isn't and we are going to have the perfect Christmas together. I've already bought his presents," I say smugly.

"Did you buy us anything?" Jake asks, his eyes suddenly sparkling. He's a big child really.

"No you didn't get shit," Carol says, half seriously. I giggle at Jake's face.

"Of course, I got you something," I say, messing up his hair while he grunts in annoyance.

"A sex doll," Carol says.

"I'm not that desperate," Jake says.

"Yes you are, you were chatting up Pat," I say, and giggle.

"Ew, no way were you chatting up Pat?" Carol asks.

"Okay, yes, but in my defence, I was drunk," Jake

whines.

"Drunk or not, that is desperate," Carol says, and they start bickering until I pull a nearby cracker at them and stun them into silence.

"Well that's just rude," Jake says.

"Guys, can one of you take over from me? I want my break," I say, impatiently.

"Fine." Carol takes the hat from me. I go to the locker room, pop in for a wee and then slather my lips in a layer of lip gloss and pucker up. I get to spend my break with Luke, that's all I want for Christmas.

CHAPTER 2

I put on my beautiful cream scarf and bobble hat and head to the back of the store and into the café. I look around for Luke but he isn't here. Could he be having his break?

Lucky for me Luke only lives two minutes up the road. I love coming to Luke's little flat. It's always immaculate and stocked up with lots of food. Luke makes the most amazing food every time I stay over.

I take the spare key from under the mat and let myself in. "Luke?" I shout into an empty corridor. All the doors are shut in the rooms and I hear the TV playing in the living room.

The bedroom is next door to the living room and is firmly shut so I head into the living room. Two glasses of wine are on the table along with an empty bottle. I pick it up to check. Who has Luke had up here?

"Luke?" I say, feeling slightly bemused as I fling open his bedroom door.

"Ow," a voice on the other side says.

Luke is standing right by the door his eyes watering in pain, holding his nose from where the door hit it.

The duvet is all creased and pulled back and my fucking boss Kelly is laying there in red silky underwear.

"What the fuck are you doing here?" Luke yells.

"What the fuck is she doing here?" I look to Kelly who I've never seen look anything but smart and tidy but who now looks slightly dishevelled like they've just had sex. Oh god, they have, haven't they?

"Urn, she's sleeping here," he says stuttering.

"You fucking arsehole, you cheated on me with my boss," I screech and slam my hand into his chest. I feel the anger rise inside me and the tears come quickly.

"Well actually I don't want you working for me anymore," Kelly says. "You're fired."

The tears warm and salty fall from my eyes and I turn away. I don't need to know when or why he did this to me and luckily we didn't ever move in together. How could he do this when we've been together nearly a year?

I run out of his flat and Luke isn't even calling after me. I don't know why that makes me feel worse. I head straight back to work because I can't think of anywhere else to go.

Was I fired after today or just immediately? Whatever, I don't want to risk seeing Kelly if she has followed me. I'm not in the mood to be festive now. I feel the hate rising in my chest and I start shaking. I haven't done anything and now I have no boyfriend and I'm jobless. How can I afford Christmas?

"Holls?" I hear Jake say and walk more quickly into the locker room. Luckily he isn't allowed to come in. I don't need to hear *I told you so* right now. I sit on the floor next to my locker with my head in my hands. When I came in this morning I was full of festivities and now I have nothing.

"Holly Jane Willow get your Santa arse out here, now." I hear over the intercom and look up. Jake did that. He knew Kelly wasn't here. If only he knew what Kelly was doing.

"No," I yell to no one in particular.

"Holls?" Carol swings open the door and sees me in a crumpled mess. My sparkly Christmas jumper now has snot and mascara all over it.

"Did they cancel Christmas?" she asks, sitting next to me.

Jake appears at the door while it's still open.

"What happened?" she asks.

"Luke," I say between attractive gulps, trying not to choke on my tears.

"What's the bastard done now?" Jake asks. The

frown lines deepen on his face.

"I caught him in fucking bed with Kelly," I cry.

"Our Kelly?" Jake asks and I nod.

"That's okay, you'll find someone else," Carol says, stroking my hair. I lean on her feeling like shit. I'm sure I've covered her uniform in mascara.

"It's not just that," I croak out. "She fired me on the spot when I saw her."

"She can't do that," Jake says, banging his hand on the wall.

"She did," I say.

"Well she isn't here at the minute," Carol says.

"She wants me out immediately," I say. Carol gives me a tissue and I blow my nose.

"I knew she was a nasty cow," Jake says with a snarl and I shake my head.

"Why don't you talk to her?" Carol says in a reasonable voice.

"I can get her back for you?" Jake offers.

"How?" Carol asks.

"I have ways," he says.

"It's okay, I'm going to go home and..." I stop myself.

What do I do? Sit and wallow at home? Think about the many times Luke's been to my house and how everything reminds me of him.

"What?" they both say looking at me.

"I can't go home. Not when everything reminds me of Luke," I blubber.

"So what are you going to do?" Jake asks.

"I'm going to stay in a hotel for a couple of days," I say but even saying it I don't feel confident. Can I even afford it?

"Will you be okay?" Carol asks.

"No, but I'm going to enjoy being pandered to for the next few days," I say.

CHAPTER 3

I arrive home to my dreary flat. It used to be full of life. I'd get home on the first day we were allowed to wear Christmas jumpers at work and immediately put up my tree with Wham! in the background and break out the mince pies. It's almost become tradition for me but today I feel deflated, like Christmas is already going to be awful. I don't feel like putting the tree up, I don't want to hear George Michael's whining about last year I want to sit and eat until I can't feel my legs and I need rolling out of the door.

I really don't want to be in this flat. The trouble is where can I go? Mum and Dad have gone away for a month and I don't really have any other family. My neighbours are either snobs or elderly so I don't want to bother them.

I absent-mindedly throw a bunch of clothes into a suitcase. I have no money so I have no idea what I'm going to do.

I chuck in my phone charger and my phone that has begun pinging. I know Jake and Carol are worried but they shouldn't be. I'm going to have a stress-free Christmas. Cameron Diaz had a Christmas alone and that went well for her though I doubt I'll find my own Jude Law this year. I need to make a resolution before Christmas to just pack in men. Maybe I'll become a nun.

I ignore my phone and walk around the house turning the switches off. I don't need to use my electricity if I won't be home and it's a waste if it's on. I drag my almost overflowing suitcase out of the door. I hear Fairytale of New York coming out of my neighbour's house.

The sky is turning a darker grey and it looks like it's going to get dark even though it's only three pm. I unlock my car and push the bulging suitcase into it. I get in the car feeling slightly better that I'm not stuck within the four walls anymore. I need to get away from life for a bit.

The rain comes down hard as I stall the car and eventually stop. I'm on a country road. I have no idea where I am and it's starting to get dark. What the fuck do I do? The car isn't working and I have no idea how to get home. I put my head on my wheel feeling like shit. God, I wish I had something to drink.

I hit the wheel feeling frustrated and the car moves towards the roundabout ahead. Little splats of rain appear on my window and I activate the window wipers as I wind my window down. The sign says my hometown is only three miles away but in the opposite direction only one mile away is a village called Christmas.

I start the car over and over until it comes to life. Oh, maybe my luck is finally changing. Curiosity has the better of me and I follow the road signs to the Christmas village, Maybe they will have a hotel I can stay in.

I drive into the middle of the village square that's lit up with rows of shops and what looks like a hotel on the corner. A sign tells me that Holy Cow Farm is up the hill. No one here knows me. They have no idea my boyfriend slept with my boss.

My car stalls and puffs out and when I try to restart it the ignition doesn't come on. Great, I will have to park here then, wherever here is. I get out into the now torrential rain. A sign outside the hotel says it's called Room at the Inn.

Should I go in? I really can't afford it but I still need somewhere to stay. If they all love Christmas maybe they can help me out?

I walk in and it's really small but the inside is decorated head to toe in Christmas. Before-Luke-cheated-on-me me I would be thrilled. I feel like I've stepped onto the set of a hallmark movie. There's even a turkey walking around the foyer. Wait, a real turkey? Should I say something to someone?

"Hello dear." A voice behind me makes me jump and a lady with rosy pump cheeks and a Santa hat greets me. She has piercingly blue eyes.

"Hi," I say with a shiver. All this rushing around means I've forgotten my coat.

"Do you need somewhere to stay?" she asks.

"Yes please," I say."But I don't have any money..."

"Mum," a voice behind me says. I spin around and a tall man looks stern while two little blonde girls are dancing around his legs. He has a frown on his face but as soon as our eyes meet he smiles at me.

"Joseph, I'm just dealing with a guest," she says, huffing with her hands on her hips.

"We have a situation at the bakery," Joseph shouts.

The woman looks at me and smiles. "This is my son, Joseph, I'm Ivy," she says and we shake hands. "What situation?" she asks turning to Joseph.

"Mrs Baker has quit," he whispers.

Ivy turns back to me looking stressed. "What was it you were saying?"

"I need a room but I don't have any money," I say. I feel so embarrassed to have just arrived here like this.

"Hello," Joseph says to me and I catch his eyes twinkling at me. They are a beautiful blue colour. His little girls have stopped running around him.

"Hi, I'm Holly," I say and we shake hands.

"I'm sure we can come up with some arrangement my dear," Ivy says handing me a key. She must feel sorry for me. God knows what I look like.

"Welcome to Christmas village," Joseph says. I smile awkwardly. Oh god, he is definitely like the picturesque Hallmark guy with the honey-brown hair. A curl of it feathers upwards and his smile makes my heart flutter.

"Thank you," I say flustered. I feel my cheeks redden. Oh god, what is wrong with me? I leave in a hurry, forgetting my suitcase and having to go back for it. Joseph watches me whilst trying not to laugh. I can't even do it cutely either because I'm pretty sure I still look a mess from this morning's crying. I didn't remove my makeup and I'm still wearing my Christmas jumper. So much for 'holly jolly' Christmas. Carol bought the jumper for me a couple of years ago because it has my name on it, I'm not feeling so jolly now though.

"Welcome to Room at the Inn. You get yourself a good sleep and tomorrow we will talk about payments," Ivy says.

I head up to my room. My key has a little elf on it and I look for numbers. Instead, I am met with a big elf painted on the door. The door next to mine is a Santa.

I unlock the door and it's like Christmas threw up everywhere. Anywhere that could be decorated is. There are garlands and wreaths around the window, a little Christmas tree in the corner next to where the kitchen appliances are and my bedspread has little happy cartoon elves on it. This should be my dream but I'm not in the mood. I could do with a drink and a good sleep.

I put my suitcase under the bed and head to the kitchen. On the side is everything to make a 'festive hot chocolate' including some generous little bottles of Baileys and Buck's Fizz. Bingo!

A knock on my door interrupts me from pouring the Baileys into a glass and I turn around with it in my hand.

"I'm sorry to bother you I just wanted to make sure you're okay dear?" she asks. She looks genuinely worried for me and my lip wobbles. I can't start crying in front of this stranger.

"Yes, I'm having a bit of a wobble," I say. If I'm not careful everything will spew out. She looks like a 'tell me all of your worries over a cup of tea' type of woman.

"Oh, dear aren't we all? But it's almost Christmas. Christmas is all about happiness and forgiveness." She lingers and I down the bottle of Baileys.

"My family are on holiday and I'm not forgiving my boyfriend. Well, ex-boyfriend," I say. I open the Buck's Fizz. Party for one and maybe some crisps. I would love a huge tub of Pringles about now.

"There must have been a reason you came to our

little village. Maybe we can help each other while you are here," she says with a smile.

I nod. "Yes I can do that. What do you need help with?"I ask.

"Don't worry about it tonight, like I said we will discuss it in the morning but Joseph will be here to help me out if there's anything you want," she says.

 "Can I have some food?" I ask. I realize I haven't eaten all day today.

"Of course," she says and disappears.

CHAPTER 4

I vy seems like the kind of person with a vegetable patch. When she comes upstairs with the nicest-smelling cottage pie in the world.

I feel a lot more relaxed and the thoughts of Luke are slowly disappearing. I look outside my window and the square is silent. The Christmas lights are still draped around the streetlamps and across the shop roofs.

I should ring Carol and Jake to let them know I'm okay. I didn't expect to find anywhere this quickly but here I am in Christmas village. I think Carol and Jake will think I'm drunk when I tell them.

"Where the fuck are you?" is screamed down the phone as soon as Carol answers the phone. Jake is swearing in the background too.

"I'm in a village called Christmas," I whisper. For some reason, I feel self-conscious and get changed for bed in the bathroom, even though I'm alone here.

"Are you hurt? Do you need us to pick you up?" she

shouts down the phone. They've clearly had a few drinks.

"Found a hunky man in a plaid jacket yet?" Jake slurs down the phone. My mind immediately goes to Joseph. I shake the thought away.

"Zero men," I quote Kate Winslet. "Just a nice old lady letting me stay in one of her rooms."

A knock on the door disturbs us and I put the phone to my chest.

"Sorry my love," Ivy pops her head around. "I made too many mince pies if you would like one," she says producing a plate with a mince pie on it. She leaves them on the bed.

"A strange old lady that gives you food?" Carole whispers.

"Count me the fuck in," I hear Jake say.

"No, guys, I really want to take this time away to relax a little and think about what I'll be doing with my life," I say.

"We'll miss you," Carol says.

"I won't," Jake says.

"I know, I miss you," I say. My eyes fill up as we say goodbye. I've not had nearly enough to drink for this emotion. Everything that has happened today has finally got to me.

I spend the next hour crying on my bed. Not just crying but howling. I could rival any werewolf in the vicinity. Even Ivy has left me to it. I cry until I pass out from exhaustion.

I wake up the next morning feeling groggy. Oh god, where am I? I sit up in the plump bed. I'm not at home. Where am I? Who am I? Then the memories come flooding back from yesterday. Luke and Kelly are in bed together. I've got no job and no boyfriend.

"Hello?" a male voice says outside. I check to see if I'm dressed and I am. A head pops around.

"Hi, I'm completely sorry for barging in like this. Oh god, I really am. My mum wants to talk to you. I wanted to make sure you're okay? She said she heard howling last night." Joseph is standing in front of the door now with his hands over his face. My face is bright red and could probably be seen from Mars.

"Oh god," I mumble, hiding my face.

"I will take that as you are okay. Well, if you fancy it, there's breakfast downstairs. Me and the girls are having some and you're welcome to join us. Not as a date obviously but as a guest," he says. He is clearly as embarrassed as I am. *Please just leave.* I think to myself.

I want to say I don't feel like a guest since I am not paying but he scrambles out of the room.

I shower and dress in one of my favourite Christmas jumpers with fluffy red bits on it and a yellow star and head downstairs. I'm not entirely sure where I'm going but I follow the waft of bacon and find Ivy, Joseph and the girls sat at the table. I feel like I'm interrupting a family moment.

"Hello, please forgive me for being a..." he whispers and I smile.

"It's okay," I say and sit down with them.

"Good morning Holly, now sit down. I want to talk to you about an issue that has risen and I think you might just be our girl," Ivy says putting a glass of orange juice in front of me alongside, an old-fashioned tea pot with a red spout and patchwork pattern in red and green at the bottom. Very Christmassy.

"That sounds great," I say. I feel a little nervous about the whole thing. What could possibly have happened that I can help with?

"My daddy says you are a part werewolf and if I'm not good you will eat me," the little girl with the golden hair interrupts my thoughts looking up at me. Her big blue eyes look slightly bewildered. I look to Joseph.

"It was a late night and they were asking about the noise," he whispers. "By the way this is Seren and this is Star."

"It's lovely to meet you but I'm so sorry to

disappoint you, I'm not a werewolf," I say to them.

"Are you daddy's girlfriend?" they ask.

"Have you come to save our Christmas play?"

I'm bombarded with questions from the two very eager four-year-olds on either side of me. I'm the shiny new toy at the moment.

Joseph looks at me with his piercing blue eyes. "I'm sorry for the spotlight questions," he says.

"It's okay," I laugh. "I am no one's girlfriend anymore," I say to the girls and I see their shoulders slump. "And I have come to help Grandma Ivy out." I catch Ivy's eye and she smiles at me.

"Is that why you came here, to get over someone?" Joseph asked.

"Yes, I needed to get away from my four walls.. My car stalled when I arrived here and then I realised too late I don't actually have the money to stay here and, well, I got a little drunk," I say.

"Let's talk about my little problem then. So it seems our baker has left the little bakery on the square and well we need someone to replace her," Ivy says.

I nod but in my head I'm screaming 'Tell her you aren't a baker. You can't do this!'

I spoon sugar and milk into my cup. Can I do this? Just because I've never really baked it does it mean I can't try? I need to pay Ivy somehow and this could help both of us like she says.

"So, what do you say?" Ivy asks me.

"If she needs a job I wouldn't mind help on the farm," Joseph says.

"I think the bakery is more in need of someone right now and anyway get your father to help you," Ivy says.

"Dad's busy in his workshop," Joseph says.

"He makes toys in his workshop for the village toy shop," Ivy fills me in.

"Yes, you know what he's like when he's in there," Joseph says.

" I used to work in a Christmas shop," I say.

"Wow," Joseph says.

"Great, so you have some retail experience. I'm sure you'll be fine," Ivy says.

"I have to go and milk the three wise cows," Joseph says.

"Are they really called that?" I say with a giggle.

Of course." Joseph smiles at my amusement.

"We are the village called Christmas, anything is possible," Ivy says. I sip my tea. Maybe this is my kind of village. I just need to channel my inner Christmas spirit. Why should I let Luke ruin it?

CHAPTER 5

As I sit and think of Luke, I realise this change could do me good. Maybe I will take new skills back home with me and that way I can find another job. For however long I'm here I can just start again clean and fresh. I really enjoyed breakfast with Ivy and her family. I can imagine having more breakfasts with them. If I'm earning my keep I won't have to leave just yet.

I'm also intrigued by Joseph. Is he a single dad? Does he have a wife or girlfriend that works away a lot? It's not really any of my business and yet I'd love to know.

After offering to clean the breakfast things and being told to go and visit the bakery, I get myself ready to face the problem. I really want the other villagers to like me.

I step outside the doors of the hotel and I'm already on the square. The little lines of shops surrounding the square look even daintier and neater than I remember. The old-fashioned lamp posts, two opposite each other are very dimly lit as the sky wakes up for the day. It must still be early.

Across from the hotel on the very end of the other side of the square is the bakery. A building with the sign 'All You Need is Cake' on it. As I walk closer I can see the red chairs and wooden tables inside.

I step inside and no one is there. The counters and floor are coated with dough. "Hello?" I shout over the counter. I hear the radio playing music in the background.

The door opens and I turn around. Joseph is standing behind me. Did he follow me? Do I want him to be here? Yes, I do.

"Hi, I have no idea what I'm doing by the way," I say, making conversation.

"You are actually a huge help to Mum right now doing this. Our baker, Mrs Baker – I know, what an original name – left last night," Joseph says.

"I am really pleased I can help I just don't really bake so I don't even know if anything I make will be edible," I say.

"Well, I'm sorry I can't be much help. Mum sent me here to give you some ingredients and some Dutch courage. You can do this," he says and smiles that smile again. I can't help whatever it is I feel. Joy? I'm not really sure but surely I don't already have a crush on the farmer?

"Oh, and you already have a hungry mob outside."He nods towards the door and I already see a little queue forming.

"They are all expecting baked goods?" I ask. He has already left before I finish the question.

I feel the pressure building. I have no choice and I don't want to let anyone down. I don't know these people from Adam but I really want Ivy to like me. Of course I also want to repay her for her kindness. I put on the 'All I Want for Christmas is Baked Goods' apron and turn up the radio.

I think the first thing on the agenda is cleaning up. It looks like a bakery bomb hit this place.

The crowds outside have become rowdy as I turn the sign to open. It's now seven am and I have no idea what I'm doing or if I did anything right, but I have cinnamon buns and mince pies in the oven. The kitchen is a mess and half-burnt goods are stacked up. I'm hoping the ones in the oven right now turn out well otherwise the crowds won't be happy.

I'm covered in flour and all sorts of the mixture as the customers pile into the shop and give me their demands. I need to thank Ivy and Joseph for giving me some paper recipes and a plan of what to make first.

I go to check on the mince pies and they smell amazing. I feel pride rising in me. My first batch of mince pies are looking good. Did Mrs Baker normally have everything organized by now? It's best not to think about that.

"Excuse me, when are we supposed to receive our mince pies? You know I'm a very busy man, I do not have time for this," a customer in a business suit says to me.

"Urm, two minutes," I say, flustered. I pull out golden mince pies from the oven. They are cooked. Thank god. I let them cool down while I pull out some of the bread from the proof drawer.

"I am so sorry urm, Mr.." I ask.

"Mr Tree, Christmas," he introduces himself and I have to bite my lip to stop giggling. Everyone is so strange in this little village almost cartoon-like. Mr Tree is tall with his grey suit practically hanging off of him on his slim frame. His glasses are perched on the end of his nose and his face is slowly turning the colour of the red tiles on the floor.

"Mr Tree, I am the new baker, well the new guest here and well, I didn't expect to be baking today so I'm sorry if I'm a little behind," I say hoping he won't be too angry with me.

"Oh, I'm sorry," he says, his voice not as rough. The other villagers also stop and it's like everyone is frozen. "What's your name then?" he asks peering down his nose at me.

"I am Holly Willow, I've come here to spend Christmas because my arsehole of a boyfriend slept with my boss," I say. "Now I am trying to help out Ivy as I'm broke but I don't appreciate being spoken to like that," I say jabbing his suit with my doughy finger. I am probably out of line but this morning is anything but relaxed.

"So you don't know Mrs Baker?" one of the villagers asks. I shake my head.

"Oh my, poor love," the girl says. She looks about my age with her long red hair in curls around her very pale face.

"I don't want sympathy, believe me," I say.

"Of course not, but you can rant to me anytime you like. My name is Angel," she says sticking her hand out.

I shake it feeling a little thankful that I might have made a friend.

"I work at the toy shop next door. Ivy, the woman you're staying with, her family run the toy workshop," she says.

"Great," I say.

"Well, coolio and hey, it might not seem much but I think you are doing an ace job," she says and smiles. I hand out the now-cooled mince pies and the crowds cut down in size. Mr Tree even compliments my mince pies.

"Yes," I scream into the air when the shop is empty. I've managed to keep the bakery going on my own and I haven't started a fire or burnt too many mince pies.

I dance around the kitchen and hear a gobbling noise outside. What the fuck?

I open the door, putting the stopper in the way and that same turkey is walking towards the door. I knew I didn't imagine him last night.

"Shoo," I say and look out to see if anyone can see it. No one is paying attention. I see villagers I don't recognize going into each other's shops and now a Santa has appeared in the middle of the square with a bucket singing 'Santa Claus is Coming to Town.'

In the distance I see a tractor racing down the road. I can't see who it is but maybe there's more to this village than I thought. I roll my eyes and grab a few gingerbread crumbs and sprinkle them on the floor for the turkey. It immediately starts bobbing towards the crumbs and pecking at them.

Feeling satisfied the turkey won't come back in, I get to icing my gingerbread people and giving a couple of them special features. I give them hair and little gem sweet buttons I found in the pantry and two of them have pretty dresses on.

I put them on display and sit down. Icing and baking are hard work

"Holly, Holly," two voices interrupt my sit down and I walk over to the display. Joseph is standing there with the two girls.

"What is it?" I ask folding my arms and looking from one to the other.

"Did you see a turkey about this big?" he asks showing me with his hands. "This tall?"

I point to the front of the bakery where the turkey is walking around pecking the ground.

"Gobble Di Gook," one of the girls says, running towards the turkey.

"Is that your turkey?" I call after him with my arms crossed. No one else seems bothered in the least that a turkey is bobbing about. Joseph scoops it up and brings it over.

"Oh yes, his name is Monsieur Gobble Di Gook," Joseph whispers. I giggle and pat his head.

"I've never stroked a turkey before," I say.

Joseph looks at me like I've said I've never eaten chicken before, shaking his head. "You haven't lived then." He winks.

"Right girls, into the tractor. We need to drop you off at school," Joseph calls. The girls stop running around and get into the tractor. This morning is turning into the weirdest morning of my life.

"I'll try to stop Monsieur bothering you again," he says and I feel disappointed. Of course he doesn't want to bother me. He doesn't even know me.

I wave them off before heading back into the shop. I think it's coffee time.

CHAPTER 6

By the time I finish making everything on the list Ivy has given me I see the early signs of sunset and sigh. For someone that'd never baked in my life, I don't think I've done a bad job.

I look at the array of decorations as I sip my coffee with a hint of caramel syrup in it. I could do this but do I really want to?

I think about it. Maybe Luke cheating on me isn't a curse and more of a blessing. I want to find out more about the people in this strange village. It feels more like home than mine ever did. Would I be able to just pack up and leave my life and just live here?

"Holly, what are you doing here still?" Angel comes flouncing in dressed in a winter coat and scarf. I feel the cold wind rushing in as the door is flung open.

"I've only just finished baking," I say. I'm more exhausted than I've ever been in my life. I feel like I have dough where dough shouldn't be.

"Would you like to come to the Christmas fete tonight? Mrs Baker had a stall but it's up to you," Angel says.

"Yes, okay then," I say, helping Angel who is picking up trays of my baked goods. "So do I sell my baked stuff and then go home?" I ask.

"Yes, basically," Angel says with a smile. I help her load the car.

"Do I have a chance to change?" I ask, still wearing my apron.

"Nope we are going to be late if we stop," she says.

I follow her to the van parked outside. It has Rudolph's Toy Box written in red letters on the side of it.

I get in the van next to her and buckle myself in.

"What's with the van?" I ask.

"It's the toy shop near the farm where Ivy and Nick live and run. I help out when I can," she says.

Angel just has such a friendly, wholesome face. Her cheeks are red and shiny and she looks like she could be an elf. She would have fit in well at Kelly's shop. I should check out the toy shop when I get the chance. My stomach is churning as we get closer to the school. The country road signs all point one way and we stop outside a one-story school that looks more like a large bungalow. The bricks are red and the playground isn't much bigger than the square all of the shops are on.

"It's tiny," I whisper, looking out of the window.

"Yes, it's a really small village. There's not even a hundred children here," Angel says.

"Thank you Holly for agreeing to help us out." Mr Tree comes out of the school gates towards the van.

"I'm sorry I didn't know about the fete," I mumble like a naughty school child.

"No one told poor Holly, Chris," Angel says.

Chris's face softens and for a minute I think he's going to say something nice when we open the back of the van at the goods all stacked up nicely.

"Yes... Well get in there or you'll miss it," he says.

We carry trays through the school reception into the main hall opposite. The reception smells like school dinners. There are other stalls dotted around selling toys and games. We take our trays to the back of the hall against the stone wall and I lay them out. Angel brings out some red and white striped bags and hooks them on the stall.

I sit down feeling anxious and nervous. I really need to work through my new hatred of Christmas though. I've always loved Christmas. I used to love volunteering at the local school to help in the festive season. The kids are always excited and there's so much to do. I am the queen of Christmas... or so I used to be. I shouldn't let Luke ruin it for me.

"Penny for your thoughts?" Angel asks. She comes over with a beautiful little boy with brown hair. He looks the same age as Joseph's girls.

"I was just thinking that I shouldn't let my ex ruin Christmas for me," I say.

"No, you shouldn't," she says.

Angel's little boy smiles at me from behind his mum's back.

This is Jude," she says stroking his hair.

"Hi, Jude, would you like some gingerbread?" I ask and he nods.

"I'll pop the money in the pot, you just pick what you want," Angel says to Jude. Jude picks what he wants and I put it in the bag for him. He happily munches it as he goes off to one of his friends.

I see Joseph walk in and I have to make myself not look at him. He looks so lovely with his brown hair and suede jacket and jeans.

The girls are running rings around him. Mr Tree is racing around telling everyone what to do.

"Hello, Angel. And you are?" A lady comes over to me with blonde hair, leggings and trainers.

"This is Holly," Angel says. I shake hands with her as she tells me her name is Melanie.

She follows my gaze. "That's Joseph but I wouldn't bother, he doesn't get involved with anyone."
"Oh no, I wasn't. I was just happy to see a familiar

face," I say, blushing. Oh, for goodness sake, I need to get myself together.

"He is gorgeous though," Angel says.

"I can't go there, I've just broken up with my boyfriend, I'm so off men," I say flustered. I'm desperate to come up with something to change the subject. I'm so embarrassed. Thank god he hasn't come over.

"That's more of a reason to go for it," Melanie says and winks.

"I'm going to get a drink," I say. Angel agrees to stay with the stall and I go off to find a lovely chocolate fountain and a tea and coffee maker. This is perfect.

"Hi, can I help you?" a friendly enough man asks me.

"Can I have a hot chocolate?" I ask and watch him heat up the fountain. It whirls around stirring in silky-looking chocolate and then tops it with cream and marshmallows.

"Thank you," I say and pay him. I head back to the stall through the now crowds of people.

"Holly?" a voice behind me says and I spin around to face Joseph.

My hot chocolate tips all over both of us and I feel the burning through my jumper.

"Oh, hey. I'm so sorry," Joseph says lifting his shirt.

I see the tiny bit of skin and can't help but look.

"No, it was my fault I'm so sorry, I heard my name and whizzed around," I say. I'm already turning bright red. I dumped my hot chocolate all over the best-looking man in the room.

"Totally my fault, I didn't expect to see you tonight, I mean, not like you aren't welcome of course but..." He trails off, reddening. His constant blush is adorable and I wonder why he hasn't bothered with anyone and what his history is. No one talks of a wife and he has never said anything.

"At least we smell good," I say, breaking the tension and he smiles.

"Yes, we do. Let me buy you another one," he says. I look over at Angel and Melanie who are gawping at me. I bat them away and roll my eyes.

"At least let me help you with that." Joseph grabs a lot of tissue and starts dabbing at my wet jumper.

"Thank you," I say.

"So what I actually meant earlier was it's pretty damn cool you're here."

I blush deeply. "I like this village, and I really want to help your mum out. Plus it's taking my mind off of my arsehole ex-boyfriend," I say. It still feels like there's a dagger in my heart.

" What did he do?" he asks and he genuinely looks interested in what I say. Is this man for real?

"He slept with my boss," I answer. I swallow the lump in my throat. Am I upset or angry? I don't want to be either. I really need to enjoy my Christmas.

"Really?" he asks and sounds surprised. "What a douche, he couldn't have picked anything more cliché."

I wonder what he knows about clichés. "Yes he's a walking arsehole cliché," I say and Joseph smiles.

"Well, it's better that you came to our village then. We can show you a good Christmas," Joseph says.

"Well, I'm here helping out at the bakery so who knows how long I will be here for," I say.

Joseph sits down and I do the same. The hall is full of parents and children and I see my own stall is doing well enough. Thank god for Angel.

"You know, a few of our villagers came here stuck with their lives and ended up staying because they liked the simplicity of our village more than their old lives." Joseph looks up at me and his blue eyes are intense. To me, they looked like deep pools of water. I need to not fall in love with a guy I won't see ever again after I go home.

"Really?" I ask.

"Yes, I've lived here all of my life with Mum and Dad and then the girls came along and we've seen villagers come and go. Each of them has got something out of being involved in our village."

"So you think I should stick around even after I've paid off Ivy?" I ask.

Baking for the village has caused a warm feeling in my stomach that my old job never did. Maybe it's the hard work but I'm enjoying my time here.

"If you want to." Joseph shrugs and smiles.

"Dad!" I hear a scream and feathers piled up on the floor.

Monsieur Gobble Di Gook is running around like crazy while Mr Tree and the other adults are trying to catch him.

I watch the madness as I think about what I want from the village. Why did I come here?

CHAPTER 7

After Gobble Di Gook is captured and Ivy takes him back home, Mr Tree gathers us around.

"Now to announce the winner of the tombola," he says, picking out a piece of paper from a hat. Everyone watches while I stand by my bakery stand nibbling on a corner of gingerbread.

"He so likes you," Angel whispers. She didn't buy a ticket either. She said it was a rubbish waste of time and the 'yummy mummies' always win.

"No, he doesn't." I bat away the look she's giving me.

"Hot guy calls out your name and spills your hot chocolate all over him. I'm surprised he didn't say let's go back to mine and I'll give you a new shirt," she says.

"This isn't Notting Hill," I say and smile. I think about if he did invite me to his. I've seen the farmhouse at the top of the hill. It's massive.

"Joseph Claus," Mr Tree says.

I perk up and look for him in the crowd.

"OMG, you like him too?" Angel says and I shush her.

"I don't even know the guy, and anyway I'm off men at the minute." I pile another gingerbread in my mouth with disgust.

"That's such a clichéd line," Angel says.

Joseph comes over with a grin on his face and a box of what looks like whiskey and other booze.

"Hi." I smile a little too enthusiastically.

"Hi, I know this is a bit forward, but would you like a drink?" he asks. I almost step on Angel's toe to stop her from saying anything.

"Yes," I say trying not to choke on gingerbread.

"Go, I'll tidy up," Angel says, shooing me out.

Joseph grabs the girls and we all head outside into the cold.

A cheery man with a white beard and rosy cheeks steps towards me.

"That's my dad Nick," Joseph says.

Come on everyone, into the van." Nick says. When he sees me he shakes my hand. "Hello, my love, are you new to the village?"

"Hi," I say and smile at him. He has a twinkle in his eye like I could tell him anything. I understand where Joseph's kindness comes from. "Yes, I'm staying for Christmas," I say.

"Well we will make it the jolliest Christmas this side of Europe," he says with a wink.

"Dad, this is Holly," Joseph says.

The inside is like a diner. 'Wonderful Christmas Time' is playing and tinsel and lights are strung everywhere. It smells like mince pies too.

"Wow," I say, looking around. If I wanted mobile Christmas this would be the place for it.

"Do you like my little Betsy?" Nick asks.

"Oh, Dad," Joseph looks embarrassed.

"Yes I like Betsy," I say and sit down next to Seren and Star.

"Can I interest you in a hot chocolate with cream and sprinkles?" Nick asks all three of us.

"Yes," we say enthusiastically and Nick chuckles. Joseph slides in beside us.

"Your family love Christmas?" I whisper.

"Something like that, yes," Joseph says.

"I used to love Christmas," I say with a smile and a sigh.

"Used to? Were you one of the crazy people who could rival Danny DeVito in 'Deck the Halls'?" Joseph asks.

"Not quite, though at work I was always the one who dressed the tree and I would be the first in line to sing for our charity event that we used to collect money for and.."

"You sang in front of people?" he asks.

"Yes," I say. I feel the excitement I used to feel when I think about my job. I loved it so much. What would I do when I got home after Christmas?

"Wow maybe you should be in charge of the class nativity," Joseph jokes.

"Why?" I ask. I feel the tingly feeling again that I felt after a hard day at the bakery.

"Because Seren and Star are doing their nativity and they are asking for volunteers," Joseph says.

I play with the handle of my cup and scoop off the layer of cream, eating it from the spoon.

"Now, Joseph, Holly is doing enough for us here as it is," Nick cuts in.

"All work and no play makes Holly a dull girl," Ivy says.

"I know but I am so grateful to be able to help you all out. I just don't know what I'm going to do with myself after Christmas," I say.

"The option's there to help with the nativity and as far as I know no one else has taken on the role," Joseph says with a shrug.

"Well, darling, you wouldn't know that, you don't really talk to the other parents," Ivy says and puts her arm on Joseph's shoulders.

"Dad, can we watch Frozen when we get home before bed?" Seren asks Star jumps around shouting, "Please!"

Joseph looks at me.

"What do you think Holly? Would you like to have a glass of brandy and watch Frozen with us?" Joseph asks. Ivy and Nick excuse themselves and I look at the two four-year-olds using puppy dog eyes to beg me.

"Please," they say over and over again.

"Sounds amazing," I say and they both scream.

"I watch it with them every night," he whispers and I giggle.

I perch on the girls' canopy beds with Elsa bedding on. Twinkly fairy lights are all around us and Joseph has brought milk and cookies for the girls.

"Daddy, can you get in with us?" I help Joseph push their beds together and he gets in next to them.

"Milk and cookies for you too." Joseph winks at me and I take mine.

"Holly, get in the blanket." Seren lifts the blanket and I take my shoes off before getting in the bed.

"Thank you," I say to both of them.

We don't even get to 'Let It Go' before the girls are happily asleep. I help Joseph take the plate and cups downstairs.

"I'll bring our drinks out," he says. I go to sit in the lounge. Nick and Ivy must already be in bed. It's been a long day and I let out a yawn.

"I'm sorry you had to watch Frozen," Joseph says setting down the bottle of brandy and two glasses.

"I enjoyed it actually, I don't see my family much," I say. It makes me feel bittersweet. I want to go home and cuddle my mum and dad but they are away travelling. I don't have siblings and there are no kids in the family.

"Family is my life," he says and smiles.

"To family," I say and hold my glass out.

"To family," he repeats and clinks our glasses. We are both silent as we drink.

"I'm really pleased I can help your mum out. I love the little hotel and this little village," I say. I down the rest of the warm brown liquid.

"Mum loves looking after people, so I imagine she loves having you there," he says.

"I really do want to stay for as long as I can. I've had such a shitty couple of days, and I don't even know what I'll do when I get back home really," I say.

"What have you always wanted to do?" Joseph asks and I look up at him surprised. I feel half like I'm in an interview and half taken aback because no one has ever asked me that question before.

"You mean if money was no object and I could be Cinderella?" I ask.

"Yes just without the faff of the slipper," he jokes.

"I don't know, I told you before I came here and caught my boyfriend in bed with my boss I used to work in a shop that specialised in seasonal events. Every year they would bring in sparkly Christmas jumpers and pajamas and I would think how much I want to design clothes like that and see people wearing them," I say. "I can't believe I told you that."

"Brandy does that to you," he says. I nod.

"What about you then? Have you always been the hot farmer of the village?" I ask. Oops did that slip out? I've only one glass.

"Definitely not hot," he says with a cheeky grin. "But yes, we've always lived on this farm, my dad designs toys for the shop next to yours and mum has her hotel. When the girls came along I did make my farm smaller but now it's bigger than it was before," Joseph says.

"What about the girls' mum?" I ask. "I'm sorry if this seems out of line."

"Not at all, seeing a single dad isn't normal is it? I learnt to plait hair, you know, from YouTube and my mum. And I have my nails painted hot pink," he says, showing me his nail with little flower stickers on. I giggle.

"They seem so happy," I say to him. Somehow we've managed to lie on the sofa together. I'm not entirely sure how but both of our heads are on the rest of the sofa and we are about an inch away from each other. I can smell the brandy on his breath.

"They are, well as happy as they can be," he says.

"What happened?" I whisper. I don't want to upset him as I have a feeling it isn't just as simple as she left him. My stomach starts spinning and I feel nervous about his answer.

"She died," he whispers just as softly. I don't even know the woman but I instantly feel tears trickle down.

"I'm sorry," I whisper just as softly. He turns and is now only a couple of inches from me and I look up at him. Is he going to kiss me? This is the most terrified I've ever been of someone kissing me but, at the same time, I feel excited. I lean forward to meet him and he looks pained. I swallow the lump as our lips touch and I can taste the alcohol on his breath. The kiss feels passionate. I wonder how long he has been on his own for.

Before I can even contemplate this thought he pulls away. "I'm sorry," he says. He springs up quickly and paces the floor. I readjust myself and wipe my mouth. Oh god, I kissed the farmer. Is everything going to be awkward now? I watch him pacing.

"I'm sorry," I squeak. I don't know what he wants

to hear and I don't want to complicate life for him and his girls. I know they mean everything to him.

"No, I'm sorry. Every day I've been on my own, well, with my parents but you understand what I mean. I didn't realise how lonely I actually was," he says. He sits down next to me and I don't know whether to comfort him or just leave him for a second. He looks at me his forehead wrinkling.

"I can't do relationships, I can't bring another woman into the house," he whispers playing with his fingers. I hold back the tears. I know I wasn't rejected per se but it feels like it and the look on his face makes me want to just cradle him in my arms and never let him go.

"I understand," I say. I do and I don't want to think about kissing him being the best thing I've ever done.

I want to get up and leave because I feel so embarrassed. I didn't expect to kiss him. The fluttering in my stomach feels intense. What about me? What about how I feel?

"I should go," I say and get up, grab my coat and put it on. It's only eleven pm I can still get a decent amount of sleep before work.

"Mum has made you a bed in the spare room," Joseph says and turns to me.

"Are you sure that's a good idea?" I ask. I don't want his mum and dad to think the wrong thing. It's clear he doesn't want a girlfriend no matter how deflated I feel.

"Yes, and in the morning I'll get your ingredients and take you home," he says. He sits and opens the brandy, necking it straight from the bottle.

"Do you do this every night?" I ask. I perch on the side of the sofa and watch him.

"Yes," he says and my heart twists.

"That can't be good for you or the girls," I say. I sit next to him. I want to take his drink away but I think that would be a bit much.

"Don't you talk to the other mums at the girls' school? I ask.

"No, I don't talk to anyone," he says

"Maybe that's the problem," I say and leave him to it.

I go upstairs as quietly as possible and into the room Ivy said I would have. I stay in my jumper but take my trousers off, climbing into bed. The tears come fast until I fall asleep.

CHAPTER 8

The house is loud when I wake up. It's officially the first of December and I have woken up feeling yucky. My head thumps and I put on my jeans. I look over at the clock and its half past four. Is everyone awake? Will they think we slept together? No, of course not. I'm not even sure I want to see Joseph. I've not been rejected like that in a while.

"Morning dear, Joseph is out on the farm. He says for you to join him when you get up," Ivy says.

I nod. She gives me a cup of coffee in a Santa cup and sends me out. It's still dark outside and a layer of frost makes everything sparkle. I put my coat on as I head out of the backdoor and up the path to the farm.

I hear the radio before I see Joseph as I head into the barn. Gobble Di Gook is pecking at a few crumbs on the floor.

The barn is split into sections housing different animals in there. There's a goat pen and chicken coop.

I stand by the hen house while he is inside collecting eggs and wait for him. He emerges a few minutes later and sees me. My heart jumps around in my chest.

"Hi," I say. The air around us feels so awkward.

"Oh, hey," he says and puts the eggs in a basket. "These are for you."

He hands me a basket of eggs. Our fingers touch and I feel the fizzing between us. Is it the alcohol from last night?

"Thank you, I had better be off," I say.

I don't want to linger and have to talk about last night. Does he even remember last night? I don't think I will ever recover from it. I don't know why I was so excited to be invited to his house and I definitely didn't think I would sleep with him so why is everything so strange between us today?

"Do you want a tour first? he asks and does that smile that reaches his eyes. It makes his face light up beautifully. I hope he doesn't hear how fast my heart is beating.

"Okay," I say.

I should leave. Every part of me says nothing is going to happen, that nothing should happen, so why am I so reluctant to leave?

I follow him to the goats where he puts out food for them. They lazily lift their heads but go back to snoozing. Clearly they don't have anything important to do.

We go around feeding the animals and I give the Gobble Di Gook a little stroke while he follows Joseph around.

Joseph loads bags of flour onto the tractor along with the eggs and helps me on. I sit next to him, our knees rubbing, and instantly feel nervous. We are so close to each other my entire body has come alive as our jeans touch. I wonder if Joseph even remembers our conversation last night or maybe he has blocked it out. I should do the same.

The journey down the hill takes less than ten minutes and at six am I'm dropped off. Usually I would crawl into bed and sleep for most of the afternoon after a night drinking but I can't. I'll have to manage with the brandy hangover.

I set the pre-heat temperature and bring out Ivy's notepad of recipes. I'm absolutely terrified I'll get it all wrong again but I get stuck in making mince pies first and while they cook I start preparing gingerbread mix and find a pack of paracetamol in my bag. Hopefully they will make me feel better.

The sun finally creeps up behind the village. I have twenty minutes until opening times and probably only twenty minutes until Angel comes in. Jude is with his dad so she is going to help me and no doubt she will ask about Joseph. I sigh while

George Michael sings about broken hearts. I must have bad luck with men. On a positive note, my hangover seems to be going away.

I knead the bread on the table and hear the familiar tingle of the bell.

"Whoa there, what did the bread ever do to you?" Angel asks wide-eyed. I huff and realise that I've been taking my frustration with men out on this doughy bread.

"Wait, is this about last night?" Angel asks. She has an apron on and has taken the bread away from me. "Go and get us drinks from over the road," she says.

I exit the bakery into the cold air and head straight into the coffee shop across the square. "You must be the new baker, I'm Natalie," the lady taking my order says, making my espresso with extra shots and sugar.

I'm not looking forward to being bombarded with questions about Joseph. I know it isn't my place to tell anyone Joseph's secret.

I walk into the bakery and Angel starts the interrogation.

"So why aren't you the cat that got the cream?" she asks.

I sigh and take a gulp of coffee. It's amazingly strong and sweet.

"The cat didn't get the cream," I say.

Angel puts cling film over the bread and leaves it to proof. I get the mince pies out of the oven and leave them to cool and then put the gingerbread in.

"Did the cat want the cream?" she asks and I can't help but giggle at the way she says it.

"No, yes, oh I don't fucking know. Why are men so complicated?" I ask.

"That's exactly why I'm divorced," she says and I laugh.

Angel turns the sign on the door to open and we already have a little queue outside. It's the morning and you'd think people would have better things to do with their day than wake up for bread.

"Morning girls," Ivy says, smiling as she orders her morning bread.

"Hi Ivy." I smile even though I feel so embarrassed that I kissed her son.

"Hello Mrs Claus," Angel says.

"Aren't you supposed to be at work?" Ivy asks.

"Not until eleven no, so I was just helping Holly out with the bakery," she says. I put the bread into the oven and pray that it's gone well.

"Can we go for a walk my dear?" she asks me. It feels like when Kelly used to ask one of us to come into her office and we would always mock them and tell them they were being sacked.

I look to Angel who shoos me off. I owe her big

time.

"Is everything okay?" I ask. My stomach churns and I feel a little sick. Did Joseph tell her what happened last night?

"Of course, I'm not here to lecture you about my son. What he does is his business," she says. We walk the opposite way to the farm, down the hill near to where the school is. Just before the school is a huge park that I imagine is full of dogs and kids this early in the morning.

"Okay," I say and bite my lip.

"I'm just saying please be careful with him. Did he tell you about his wife?" she asks.

"He told me she had died," I say. I don't want to think of the look on his face. So twisted and pained. I just wanted to hug him but then he sprang up and pushed me away.

"Since she died, he hasn't wanted to be close to anyone. He has continually pushed his father and I away, and won't let another woman come near him. I was surprised when he invited you to the house, and a little bit thrilled," she says.

"I don't think anything will happen," I say.

"I know he pushed you away at the first sign of a feeling but give him time, they say time is a great healer." She pauses and smiles. "Anyway, I also wanted to say to you that I'm really proud of you for stepping into the bakery role. You've been amazing with the customers and I've tasted your mince pies. I know you are paying for your hotel room and I really appreciate that so I want to invite you to stay."

"You mean stay, stay?" I ask and emphasis it.

"Yes dear, you even said yourself that you don't know what to do with yourself. I hope you consider staying because I can see you are talented and will fit in well here," Ivy says. Her eyes light up and I smile.

"It's true, I'm at a crossroad. I don't know what I will do when I go home. When I was younger I wanted to design my own pajamas and Christmas jumpers to sell but now I've lost my job, I have no hope," I say with a shrug. It will always be one of those pipe dreams.

"Well you never know, our village takes care of its community. You are already helping with the bakery so maybe we can help you," Ivy says.

I silently walk beside her until we stop. A little bridge goes over a bubbling winter lake and I sit on the edge of the bridge.

I look out into the frosty distance. If I get involved will I want to go home? Do I want to go home? I've never really known my place but I've felt more at home here than I ever did at my actual house.

"What can I do?" I ask and she smiles as we slowly walk back.

CHAPTER 9

I t's Monday morning and apart from a few pleasantries I haven't really spoken to Joseph. I do carry Ivy's words in my heart very heavily but it isn't like I want to get involved with her son. I mean, yes, we kissed, but that's it. He made it very clear and when we see each other its really awkward. Neither of us really knows what to say.

"Ah, Mr Tree, how lovely of you to drop in," I say with gritted teeth. I know he takes his head teaching very seriously but I wish he would just chill out a little. The little vein in his head looks like it could burst any second and I don't want to clean that up.

"Yes, yes. I don't have time to chit chat," he says pacing the bakery.

"Why what's wrong?" I ask. I think about Ivy's words. Could I help with a school related problem? I'm not exactly trained.

He sighs and looks at me. "I can't believe I'm gossiping, but our reception teaching assistant has been taken ill and there's no one to do the school nativity. The parent's are disappointed and the children are upset."

"Oh," I say. Ivy's words burn into my brain and I bite my lip. Is there any way he would let me do it? He doesn't even know me. I would need a background check and everything. I'm not qualified at all.

He shakes his head. "I was just thinking..." he says.

I turn away to pack up his order taking extra care. Shall I do it? Should I say yes?

"What?" I ask and turn back to him giving him his bag.

"It's daft, excuse my old brain," he says.

"Maybe I can do it," I say. I take a deep breath, wondering if I really just said that. How can I do it with the baking too?

"Can you?" he asks. His weirdly bushy eyebrows rise almost to his hair line.

"I want to talk to Ivy first," I say. If Ivy is right then everything happens for a reason. "I need the distraction."

He raises just one eyebrow this time. "Hmm, man trouble," he mutters.

"Something like that," I say.

I look around All You Need Is Cake and realise

how uninspiring it looks. Compared to the other shops that all looks like Christmas threw up all over them, this place looks like the Grinch works here. The only festive thing around here is 'Gobble Di Gook' who is inspecting the ground for any crumbs.

No wonder no one really wanted to be here. I put the closed sign on the bakery and walk into Rudolph's Toy Box and Ivy is standing at the till. Angel is crimping red decorations.

"Oh, hey, you decided to check out the toy shop after all," Angel says when I walk in.

"Well yes, but I need help with something," I say. She is dressed in a glittery Christmas outfit and a Santa hat. Decorations hang from every corner of the shop with a Christmas tree sitting in the window and snow decorations dangling from the ceiling.

"What's on the list?" she asks.

"Christmas tree, fake snow and lights," I say. I count it up on my fingers. I really need to make the little bakery look better.

"Ooh, decided to spruce up then?" she asks. "This isn't to attract the cat back is it?"

I laugh. If anyone's making me feel better then it's Angel. She is just so cheerful.

"So what's going on with you two?" she asks. She picks me out everything on my list and I follow her like a lost animal.

"I haven't seen him for a couple of days," I say.

"He's probably sulking that he pushed you away," she says.

"He shouldn't be the one sulking," I say. I feel my cheeks burning.

"He shouldn't have bloody rejected you, I mean jeez, look at you, any man would be fucking lucky to have you and he blew it." She shakes her head too.

"I don't think so..."I say, shaking my head too.

"Of course he shouldn't have. Hey, why don't you join us at the pub tonight? It's Christmas karaoke, a bit of a laugh and you can meet some of the other villagers," she says.

I nod. "Sounds amazing."

"And guess who never comes to the pub on event nights," she says nudging me with her elbow. I groan. I don't need to hear his name.

There's no queues waiting for me when I get back so I leave the bakery closed and bring out the step ladder.

"Can I help?" a voice says when I'm already taking the lights out of the box. I miss my step and fall but Joseph grabs my arm.

"Are you okay?" he asks helping me back onto the ladder.

"You distracted me," I mumble.

He flashes me a smile for a minute. "Well, I came to get Monsieur Gobble Di Gook

"He was here earlier pecking at the crumbs," I say. "But you can help me if you want."

He takes the box off me and hangs the rest of the lights up as if it's nothing. I catch a glimpse of his arse in his jeans and it's a very nice one.

"There you go," he says, stepping down the ladder.

"Thank you," I say and he is staring at me. I smile at him but feel my face heating up. I still feel really awkward around him.

"So, urm, I also came here to ask if you were going to the pub tonight?" he asks

"Yes, Angel has said they are doing something there for Christmas," I say.

"The Santa ball," he says. "I've heard its fun."

"So how come you never go?"I ask him.

"I just don't join in with the gossiping parents. I've found it's easier to just not go to events like that," he says.

The air between us feels awful. I wish it could be as easy as it was at the school.

"I think it sounds fun, urm, I probably should get the bakery open," I say and turn around, smacking my face into the door of the bakery. Oh for fuck's sake.

"Are you okay?" he asks again. I touch my nose which is pouring with blood. So much for leaving him alone.

"Oh no, let me get my first aid kit from the tractor," he says. I hold my nose and watch him run over to it and come back. His hair shines in the light from the winter sun. Why does he have to be so nice?

He tells me to hold my nose and tilt forward. I do as I'm told and feel his arm brushing mine as he stops the bleeding. That feeling I get again as if my body comes to life when he touches me. I can't believe he is looking after me.

"Sorry," I mumble. We are both covered in my blood.

"No need, I was in the right place at the right time," he says.

He looks into my eyes and I feel my breath escape me again. Whatever he is doing is driving me crazy. 'At least Angel seemed confident he would not be going to the pub tonight..."

CHAPTER 10

Before I head to the pub I nip into the hotel to talk to Ivy.

"Ivy can we talk?" I ask. She looks like she is in the middle of serving dinner.

"Of course love," she says and gestures for me to sit down opposite her.

"Ivy, I know I am helping out at the bakery right now but Mr Tree came in and was in a bit of a pickle to find someone to help out at the school. I obviously said I would talk to you first but what do you think?" I ask.

She smiles at me. "You would like to help out at the school?" she asks.

"Yes," I say with a nod.

"Let me let you into a secret Holly, it was never about the money making up for the hotel room. I think time is more valuable than money could ever be and if someone donates their time to help then that says so much about them as a person. If you want to help the school I can find someone to help with the bakery. I think it's a wonderful idea," she

says.

◆ ◆ ◆

After I finish telling Angel all about my encounter with Joseph she raises her eyebrows and shakes her head.

"You know what it is, right?" she asks.

"No, please enlighten me," I say.

"Sexual frustration from both sides," she says. I sip my drink. Oh god.

"No, it can't be." I shake my head. "He told me when he was drunk he can't be with anyone because of the girls," I say. I slink down in my seat a little. His little girls are lovely and it's so sweet that he cares but I'm so worried about him being on his own.

"Exactly, he's dying for a woman but is resisting," she says.

"Can we talk about something else?" I ask. I spot Melanie coming in with a gang of other mums, and the kids are all running riot. There's a table of food spread out for all of us and a stage is set out by the wall. It's like a party.

"Sure, but the sooner you admit it, the sooner you can do something about it," she says.

"Hi girls," Melanie says and hugs us. She smells like expensive perfume.

"Hi," I say nervously. The other two women come

over.

"Holly this is Robin and Terri," Melanie says, gesturing to each woman in turn.

"So, how are you finding the village so far?" Terri asks me. She scares me. She looks like a power mum, one of the mums I would definitely be jealous of if I was at the school gate.

"Oh I love it," I say with a smile. "I've never been anywhere like this before."

"When I was looking for somewhere to escape with my son, Nick and Ivy let me stay in their hotel until I was back on my feet. I owe them so much," she says.

I nod. "Same with us really," Melanie says.

"They gave me my job," Angel says.

"Do they own the village or something?" I ask.

"Rumour has it, Nick and Ivy lived here on their own for many years and built the entire village. Did you know they own the toy workshop and they supply the goods for the supermarket like eggs and milk," Melanie says.

"No, I had no idea," I say with a shake of my head.

"No she just wants to bed their son," Angel says. The other two laugh, and I give her the death stare.

"I do not want to bed him," I say.

"He clearly wants to bed you," she argues.

"Why, what's he said?" Melanie asks looking from one of us to the other.

"Holly got all dizzy when Joseph was looking at her," Angel says.

"I basically walked into the bakery door," I say, my cheeks flushing at the memory.

"Ooh, he has never shown interest in any of the school mums," Terri says.

"No, he hasn't. So, do you like him?" Melanie asks. I groan again.

"Seriously, can we just talk about something else?" I ask.

"Why don't we talk about the fact you have volunteered to help with the school nativity?" Angel says.

"Have you?" Melanie asks.

I nod. "But how do you know?"

"It's going around the playground. You'll find any news will do that around here," Angel says.

"That's so exciting," Terri says.

"It is, hopefully I can be helpful with it, I'm used to singing in front of people," I say. I see them looking at each other knowingly.

"Welcome, welcome, to the fourth Christmas show. Now, everyone join in whenever you want to because it just wouldn't be the same without you," a voice from the stage shouts through the microphone. "I'm Eirwen and I will be your host tonight."

Melanie springs up and before I can even know what she's doing she whispers in Eirwen's ear.

"It seems we have our first volunteers, can we have a round of applause for Joseph and Holly," Eirwen says. The disco light points at me and Melanie and Angel have to force me to get on stage. I am going to kill them when I get down.

Joseph appears on stage looking red and blotchy.

"Hi," I say and smile at him.

"Hi," he says and looks down at his feet. He is avoiding eye contact. My smile disappears and I feel the tension between us I wish we didn't have to do this.

"Now crowds, can you give them a song to sing?" Eirwen shouts to the audience.

"Oh, no, I don't really do karaoke," Joseph starts.

"Baby It's Cold Outside," I hear someone scream. The crowd cheers and I look at Joseph who looks as if he wants the ground to swallow him up.

"I can't do this," he says. He looks at me and although him biting his lip is incredibly sexy I feel almost sorry for him.

"Down this," I whisper and hand him a shot. He does what I say and takes the microphone. I know alcohol gives him a little courage because he would never have kissed me without it and we start singing.

I get really into it, dancing next to him, and the crowd roars. His lines are sung in a lot more of a whisper and he still looks terrified. When we hit the last note he grips my hand and squeezes it.

The crowd clap and I hug him, forgetting that I don't like him right now but riding on the adrenaline of having just sung with him.

"Wow, that was something wasn't it everyone?" Eirwen asks and they all cheer. We walk off the stage and Joseph hides in a booth.

I sit down next to Melanie and Angel and feel the goose bumps on my arms. I know it's just a song but it didn't feel like that to me.

"OMG you were electric out there," Angel whispers.

"I know and I think there was something between us," I say. Maybe it's still the adrenaline but I feel excited. I feel like I've just bungee jumped off of a mountain.

"You've got goose bumps," Melanie says.

"I know," I say and show my arms. Sure enough the goose bumps are still there. My heart is thumping.

"But he practically ran away like you farted," Angel says. Melanie giggles and I frown. He did run away and that hurts more than he will probably ever know.

"So, next on the stage we have two little girls, Seren and Star. And what are you singing girls?" Eirwen asks them. They look so pretty in their pink sparkly dresses and headbands.

"Santa Claus Is Coming to Town," they scream together down the microphone.

The song starts and they shout it through the microphone while jumping around. I feel a little tear in the corner of my eye and look around. I catch Joseph's eye and I smile. He smiles back and I feel it again. That electric force.

I want to invite him to sit with us but I don't think he would want to be bombarded with questions from the mums. I'm already getting enough looks from both of them. I think I need to get drunk.

"Ho, ho, ho," A voice comes from the front of the pub, holding the reins of real life reindeer. It seems I'm the only person who is a little scared of this. Seren and Star stop singing and run over to stroke them.

"Santa Claus is in town, ho, ho, ho," the voice booms. Whoever is dressed as Santa has done an incredible job. It isn't like the busker . This Santa actually looks like he could be Santa.

"Santa!" All of the kids are now dancing around the reindeer. Seren is feeding one of them a carrot and I just stand with my mouth open.

"You'll catch flies," Joseph says behind me.

"I've just never seen this before," I say folding my arms.

"The reindeer are actually staying at the farm for the rest of the month," Joseph says.

"Is one Rudolph?" I ask.

"No, silly. One's Donner and one's Prancer," he says like I should know.

"Silly me," I say and smile.

"Can we talk?" he asks and I nod. "Fancy talking in a one horse open sleigh?" My face lights up and he laughs.

I want to make a sarcastic joke but I also don't want to scare him away. I really want to tell him how much I enjoy his company.

We sit in the sleigh, which is attached to a car with rope. It feels like a kids' machine you put money into and it rocks because it's moving in the wind. I hold onto the sides as Joseph controls the Christmas music with a remote control. I wonder who is actually driving us.

"So, what is it?" I ask looking at his face. It glows from the light of the moon.

"Oh, yes, of course." He looks into the distance and I wonder if this is about the other day. Is he embarrassed? Does he even remember what he said?

"Your girls are beautiful," I say to start the conversation.

"They are everything to me," he says and he lights up, as he does whenever he talks about them.

"I understand that," I say and smile at him. I think it would be more appropriate to wear a sign saying I won't hurt you.

It's the strangest thing that I broke up with Luke and would snap Joseph up in a heartbeat. It's weird I respect him so much that I would back away if he asked, as much as it would hurt.

"I'm sorry about the other night," he says. He narrows his eyes and I feel that lump in my throat. I swallow it down.

"It's okay," I squeak. Even though it isn't I'm thankful for the darkness covering my embarrassed face.

"I don't usually try to kiss strangers," I say.

"Am I a stranger?" he asks with one eyebrow up and now it's my turn to blush.

"Well, no, not anymore," I say.

"Good, because I like you being around here. I don't know what it is but please stop me if I'm making a fool out of myself," he says. We stop outside the hotel. The music has died down.

"I like being here, I needed somewhere to come to

get away from my life and this place feels more like home than mine ever did," I say.

"Then stay, at least for a bit longer."

I swallow back the tears. Can I really promise that? "Why?" I ask.

"Because, well, because," he stutters and messes with his hair.

Instead of saying anything he leans towards me and kisses me. This time we aren't drunk and as our lips brush I feel the electric energy go through us again. I've never had a kiss like this one before.

When he pulls away I'm breathless.

"I've got school tomorrow, I should be going," I say, still feeling dizzy. He helps me out and watches me go into the hotel. He has no idea how much I want him to come in with me.

CHAPTER 11

I wake up feeling sorry for myself. Why couldn't I have been braver? I tossed and turned all night thinking that I've ruined my one chance with Joseph. Why didn't I invite him in?

"Morning lovey." Ivy comes into my room with my clean clothes. "Are you okay? You look like you didn't sleep a wink."

"I'm okay," I say though my voice betrays me. I feel sick and my stomach sinks.

"Whatever it is, it will sort itself out," Ivy says and sits on the bed.

"Will it though?" I ask. Ivy's mouth hangs open. She seems surprised I'm opening up to her.

"Of course dear," she says and smiles.

"I've found a place I feel more at home and myself than ever before and I'm supposed to leave in twenty days," I say. I sigh.

"Do you have to leave?" Ivy asks. Her blue eyes bore into me and I feel like I might melt into a puddle of tears.

"I don't know," I say. "I need to sort out my flat with my landlord. But then again I don't have anything to go home for."

"And you've just been given a job at the school. Sometimes things work out for us if we take a risk. It's almost like fate is working it's magic," Ivy says with a smile.

"But the job is only for Christmas," I say.

"But then it's time to do what you want to do, look into your heart and think about your own dreams. If staying here is what you want then do it. Life is too short to be unhappy," Ivy says and I want to hug her.

"I've never really stopped and had time to think about what I want," I say. I have always sewn my own clothes. I did textiles in college but then I got my job at Kelly's store in my last year and never saw the need to do anything with my degree.

"I can already see in your eyes that there is something you want to do, isn't there? A problem shared is a problem halved," she says in friendly tone. I always feel like I want to pour out all my secrets to her. I wonder if she's like this with everyone.

"Ever since I was little I loved designing clothes for my Barbies and teddy bears. I wanted to branch out into fashion and design my own Christmas jumpers and pajamas because I love Christmas so much," I say.

I feel like part of a weight has been lifted off me. I've put away my dreams and for what? To get sacked by my boss when it's her fault she was sleeping with my boyfriend.

"That's a magnificent gift and I'm sure we could use something just like that right here," Ivy says.

My heart quickens and my eyes light up. I feel like I've come alive again. I might live my dream finally, even if I don't get the man I want.

"Do you want me to take you to the school this morning?" Ivy asks.

"Urm, yes, if you aren't busy," I say. I did sneakily check the bus timetable and realised that not a single bus passes through the village. It's almost like it isn't on the radar.

"Of course not love, let's go," Ivy says and we walk out of the hotel and into the car park where my car is still broken down. Ivy is chatting away while we get into her car and I nod along with her.

"Would you like to stop off at the bakery for breakfast?" Ivy asks and I shake my head. My stomach rumbles in response but I can't eat. I'm way too nervous. I've never worked in a classroom before and don't have the slightest idea of what I'm doing. What if the teacher hates me?

"You need to keep your energy levels up, I suspect you will be running after children all morning," Ivy says.

"I'm so nervous Ivy, what if they don't like me?" I say, voicing my concern.

"They would be silly not to. I know the school, everyone is friendly, we aren't like anywhere else," she says.

I nod. It's beginning to feel like that here. It's the weirdest feeling to feel like I belong in this little village I've been in four days.

The journey there takes less than ten minutes and we park outside the little red brick school. I've never been more nervous about anything in my life.

"You will be absolutely fine." Ivy reassures me with a hug.

"Thank you, Ivy, for everything," I say and head inside. I wipe a tear from my eye. I've never been this emotional before. Yes, I cried when Luke cheated on me but this feels like I've really made a friend who has my back. I know she probably thinks I still really like her son and I do. I just don't know how to process these thoughts. Maybe I am blocking them out because he rejected me.

By nine am I'm sitting in the staff room. There's comfy squishy blue chairs that I want to take home with me. I'm just waiting for the children to come out of assembly while I sip my hot coffee.

I have no idea yet what children I'm looking after. Mr Tree was vague, probably in case I changed my mind. But I've agreed now and I will stick it out. I hope the school know I have no idea how to direct a nativity. Oh god, what if it's awful?

Mr Tree comes into the room dressed in a grey suit. "Ah, Holly, urm what is your last name?"

"Willows," I say and follow him through the staff room and onto the nice carpeted floor. My shoes are already rubbing against my heels as I follow him into the classroom.

"Hi Mrs Snowflake," Mr Tree says. I walk in hiding behind Mr Tree.

"Melanie?" I whisper as I look at her.

"Surprise," she says. I laugh almost hysterically. This isn't going to be as bad as I thought.

"So we haven't scared you away yet then?" she asks.

"I told Ivy I would help out at the school. I'm still repaying her back for my hotel room," I say. I wave at the kids sat on the floor.

"You are our guardian angel," she says.

I have thirty pairs of eyes on me as Melanie introduces me.

"So, we are going to be doing the nativity in just under two weeks," Melanie says. Shit did she say two weeks?

She sees me biting my lip. "Sorry," she mouths.

"We can do it, of course we can," I say enthusiastically to the children.

"We've got the scripts and the music on CD," Melanie says.

I sit with the children on the carpet even though Melanie has given me a chair. I'm bombarded with questions.

"What is your name Miss?" one of them asks. A little boy wearing glasses.

"Oh, sorry everyone, this is Miss Willows," Melanie says.

"Hello Miss Willows," they all chant back.

"Hello everyone, I'm really excited to be involved in the nativity this year," I say.

"We've got a problem," Melanie says.

"Oh?"

When I used to work at Kelly's if someone said that I would make sure I got involved and tackled the problem. Now I'm here I feel a sense of dread. The last big problem had me up at three am baking for a bakery when I had no experience at all.

"We have the script but they haven't sent us any clothes." Melanie shuffles through the enormous box labeled *nativity* with my help and all we find is a strand of tinsel that's seen better days.

"I can do the clothes," I say. I feel like I was sent to this village for a reason and this means I can showcase my talents making clothes. My insides feel alive again and I beam at Melanie. I can make the class costumes. I can get involved just like Ivy says.

"Will you have time?" Melanie asks

"Of course," I say. I can't wait to start my new project.

The children are buzzing as we start casting for the nativity. I didn't know it was this big a deal but everyone is excited.

I stand with the "Marys" as Melanie groups up all of the children into what they would like to be. Three children are left over. Dexter, Seren and Star, Joseph's girls.

"What would you two like to be?" I ask as Melanie is sorting out the children going for lunch.

"I want to be a star," Star says. I smile.

"I want to be a cow," Dexter says.

"I want to be an angel," Seren says.

"Seren, we have a group for angels why don't you stand with them?" I say pointing to the massive group of angels.

"I don't want to leave Star," she says and holds her hand.

My heart glows and I smile. "Of course you can be a star," I say to Star and she smiles and skips off to her own group.

"Class One, after lunch we will tell you what role you will be playing," Melanie says.

I help the children get their coats and line up at the door. When they've gone I'm on my own with Melanie.

"I can't believe you've only been here a couple of days and yet you've got two villagers out of a rut," Melanie says sitting down with a KitKat Chunky.

"Well, I'm here for Christmas, so I thought I might as well make myself useful," I say.

"So aren't you staying after?" she asks and I pause. I still haven't decided. Can one person just leave their life and start again?

"I don't know," I say. "I love being here with everyone but what about when the magic of Christmas ends and I'm jobless at the end of it?" I say.

"You won't be jobless; you've built up your skills at the bakery and helping here. If you make our costumes, I'm sure Nick will snap you up to work in his workshop," Melanie says.

"What does he do in his workshop?" I ask. I've seen the massive building next to the farmhouse and wondered what goes on in there. Does Nick really make the toys for the supermarket? Could my designs make it to the workshop? I shake the thought away. Of course Nick doesn't make everything and no one has even seen my designs.

How do I even know they are good enough? What if my costume designs aren't any good?

"He makes the little wooden toys in the toy shop next to the supermarket. You should go in one day and have a look around," Melanie says.

"I have but not properly," I say.

Melanie goes off to get us coffee and I take out my design book. I carry it absolutely everywhere with me. It's full of my designs and little notes of what I want to design in the future. Could my dreams come true?

My phone buzzes and a text from Kelly flashes up.

Can you come to the store? K x

I scoff. I was fired when I hadn't done anything and now she wants me back.

No. I type finally and put my phone down.

It starts ringing seconds later and I look at the screen.

Jake.

Melanie is still not back but I excuse myself and answer the phone in the cloakroom.

"Jake what is it?" I whisper. I don't know if I should even have my phone with me in the school.

"Hello to you too, Mrs Vanished-Off-The-Face-Of-The-Earth, you know, I would have sent a search party but Carol said to leave you be," Jake says down the phone. I smile. It's typical of him.

"I've been busy," I say.

"You've met a man," he corrects. Shit do I deny it? I did meet a man but it isn't like we are together.

"No, I haven't. I'm working," I say and he snorts."Anyway what are you ringing for?"

I hear Carol in the background. "Holly, Holly are you there?" Carol asks and I hear panic in her voice.

"I'm here, what's going on?" I ask. I see Melanie through the little door but she doesn't see me. She looks round for me and then sits down.

"It's Kelly, well, actually it's Luke. He dumped her and she says we need to get you back here. The place has gone to shit," Carol says.

"Oh," I say. I listen as they tell me how Kelly has gone off on one and started drinking in the store, and that management came and sacked her on the spot.

"Well, I can't come back," I say. I don't feel bad. Well, I do for my friends, I love them, but I don't for Kelly. She shouldn't be sleeping with someone else's boyfriend and whatever has happened to her she deserves.

"There's another thing," Jake says. I wait for him to carry on. "Luke wants to get in touch."
"Don't give him my number and don't let him find me," I say quickly in panic.

"We can't even find you that address you gave. It doesn't exist. It's just a field," Jake says.

"You know you can trust us, Hol," Carol says.

"I know, I will ring you when I'm not busy, I promise," I say and we say goodbye. My heart is heavy as I put my phone in my pocket. What did they mean they couldn't find where I was.

CHAPTER 12

T he afternoon goes surprisingly fast as we sort out our Mary and Joseph. We put the names in a hat and pull them out, thinking that is the fairest way to do it. I feel so bad for the other children who are disappointed when they aren't picked though.

We manage to cast almost everyone with the fewest tears (and snot) we can do before we let them out of the door for the afternoon break. Melanie is going to cut out the script for the class to take home and learn, while I measure up the children so I can make their costumes. I want to see if there's a fabric shop in the village that I can use. I feel so excited as I stand in the tiny photocopier room with the one steamed-up tiny window, photocopying the script.

"Hello everyone, hang your coats up and come and sit on the carpet," Melanie says. I come back with the script and sit down on my chair next to the class on the floor.

"Miss Willows is going to take a small group of you at a time to be measured up for your costumes, we are very lucky that we have someone special here to make our costume for us," Melanie says.

They circle me like sharks and start shouting commands of what they want.

"Can I have a pocket in my costume for my teddy?" one of them asks.

"Can mine have three heads?" Alex asks. I'm sure that's the little boy who wants to play the donkey.

"Class one, come back to the carpet," Melanie says and they join her.

I'm sent away with Mary and Joseph to measure them up. We are given privacy in one of the empty classrooms. I take the measurements with each child with wiggling and insane commands and by the time I finish I'm exhausted. I don't get how Melanie does it.

I arrive back with the last two children as Melanie is reading the class a story. We don't have long until the kids go home and I have an idea about the nativity. I want to speak to Melanie and Joseph to see if we can somehow have the nativity on the farm like the Vicar of Dibley episode - but hopefully less messy.

I help with coats and bags and all sorts of other things I didn't know children took to school with them. Half of them aren't named so they end up in a lost property box apparently. There is a shoe in the box. How does a child go home without a shoe?

I follow the line out of the door and see familiar faces. Joseph is standing outside in his red plaid jacket looking hot. I wonder what it was he wanted to say to me the other day. Obviously it isn't appropriate in front of everyone but maybe we can talk again.

As Melanie lets the kids out the door Joseph comes over.

"How did your first day go?" he asks me as he gives the girls a hug and takes their bags from them. I ignore the buzzing feeling in my hand from when our skin brushes.

"It was good. We've cast all of the children in the nativity. I was wondering if I could ask you a favour?" I say.

"Daddy, I'm the bright star that leads the wise men to the baby Jesus," Star says, beaming. She is so excited and I smile. We definitely cast her right and I will make her the best costume.

"And I'm an angel, I will have wings," Seren adds.

"I can't wait to see both of you," Joseph says proudly. He really loves his girls and it's so sweet to see all he does for them. "What was the favour?"

"Can we have the nativity on the farm?" I ask.

Joseph's face lights up. He smiles widely and says "Of course."

"Yay!" The girls jump around screaming.

"We need to make sure it's okay with the school first," I say and nod towards him.

Joseph smiles politely at me and we stand awkwardly. I want us to be more than just smiling at each other and the thought makes me blush. I really want to talk about the kiss we shared. Did it mean as much to him as it did to me?

"Let us know," he says and hovers before waving goodbye and leaving me standing next to Melanie.

We walk back into the classroom.

"He really likes you," she says as soon as we are safely back in the classroom. "Having the nativity at the farm has nothing to do with spending time with him does it?" she asks, her hands on her hips.

"No, I thought it would be cool for the children to see Jesus born in a stable, we can have real animals in the background, maybe we can supply drinks and food for it too," I say.

"It's a really good idea, you've just got to get round Chris," she says. "And bloody ask Joseph out before he finds someone else."

"I can't. He told me about his wife. I didn't want to ask when he lost her," I say. I want to know but I don't want to ask him. Would he answer the question?

"Three years ago, the girls had just turned one," Melanie says. My heart wrenches and I feel sorry for them.

"So they won't remember her?" I ask.

She shakes her head. I feel the tears in my eyes. That's so sad.

"The girls mention that their mummy is in the sky," Melanie says.

"And Joseph has been alone ever since?" I ask. She nods.

"I wish there was something I could do," I say.

"Ask him out," she says.

"I can't after our conversation the other day. He told me he doesn't date because of the girls," I say.

"Spend more time with him, get to know him and maybe it might change something. The girls love their dad but he always looks incredibly sad to me. We try to invite him to the pub but he always says no," Melanie says.

"He came the other day," I say.

"I know, we were all surprised, I still think it's because you were there," she says.

"No it isn't." I bat away her words. She eyes me suspiciously.

"You like him and he likes you, I don't get it," she says.

"Because he said..." I start.

"I know what he said but what if he changes his mind?" she asks.

"I think he's pretty insistent on this one," I say.

"No harm in asking," she replies.

I follow her around tidying up after the children.

"I really enjoyed you working here with me today," Melanie says. I smile because even though I'm exhausted and want nothing more than to jump in a bubble bath, I loved it. It's not my calling in life but I'm happy to help out with the nativity and it means I'm still paying Ivy for my room.. I'm definitely not trying to get closer to Joseph though. I respect that he wants to be a dad and that's what makes me like him so much. I feel like the other day when he pushed me away that was the real him and he hides it with alcohol and denial.

"Me too," I say before grabbing my things and going outside. I didn't think about how I would get home. I really need to get my car fixed. I sit on the wall and wonder who I can call. Its four pm and getting darker. The streetlights have already started coming on. I could walk it, I suppose. It would only be a fifteen minute walk.

The wind whips around me as I start back up the hill towards the square. I missed Mr Tree before I left but surely I would bump into him tomorrow.

Some of the shopkeepers on the square are beginning to shut down their shutters and head home. The only shops that are still open are the coffee shop, supermarket and hotel. I head inside the coffee shop and see Mr Tree ahead of me.

"Ah, Holly, good to see you, I hear you are making the costumes for the nativity?" he says. I nod.

"Yes, the children are really enthusiastic," I say and smile. I order my drink and he hovers.

"I was wondering if we could have a chat," I say.

"Of course," he says. He seems a lot friendlier than the first couple of times I've seen him and I wonder why I thought he was mean.

"Well, I was wondering if we could have the nativity at the farm?" I say.

Mr Tree's eyebrows move as he ponders the idea. "It would be educational," he starts.

"Yes, it would, and it would be realistic too with the barn," I add.

He nods. "Have you asked Mr Claus if it's okay with him?" he asks.

"Yes, he's said it's okay," I say.

"Then it's fine with me."

I throw my arms around him.

"Thank you, thank you," I say. He looks embarrassed but I smile anyway, walking out of the shop with my hot chocolate. I walk the short distance to the hotel.

A voice makes me jump. "Hello stranger." I turn and my legs feel like Jelly when I see Joseph standing on the street behind me. He's holding Gobble Di Gook.

"Hi," I say back and tuck a strand of my hair behind my ear. He seems to be everywhere I am. I would think it's creepy but this village is tiny so it isn't that surprising.

"I've just come to put Gobble Di Gook to bed but the girls have been talking about you nonstop since they got home," he says. "I wanted to find you and thank you for letting Star be the star in the nativity. I know it doesn't seem like a big deal but it means the world to me and to see them this happy makes me happy," he says. I gasp because I genuinely didn't expect him to thank me.

"You do such a good job with the girls. I loved being in their class today," I say.

We are silent and I hover outside the hotel. I don't want him to leave but I'm not sure inviting him in would be a good idea.

Ivy appears at the doors. "Ah, Holly just in time for dinner. Hello son, why don't you come in from the cold? And give Gobble Di to me."

Joseph looks like he's about to say no but gives Gobble Di Gook to Ivy and we follow her in. I want to thank her but I feel she already knows what she's doing.

She leads us through to the kitchen where there's Christmas music on in the background and two plates of dinner with two glasses of wine.

"Mum did you set us up?" Joseph asks.

"Who, me? No, of course not," she says with a smile and winks at me behind Joseph's back.

"I thought after a day of farming and schooling you would both need feeding. Your dad is feeding the animals with the girls," Ivy says.

She slips away with the turkey and I sit down.

"My mum tricked me," Joseph says. I giggle. He's a grown man and his mum has made him come here.

"I was actually just talking to Chris about the nativity," I say.

"He looks scary at first, but he's pretty decent," Joseph says. I nod and cut up my lasagne before putting it into my mouth. It's absolutely amazing.

"Chris says we can have the nativity on the farm," I say and his head shoots up. His eyes sparkle and I have to catch my breath. I feel our knees touching under the table. Why can't I ask him what I want to?

"That's great," he says.

I nod. "We are doing the traditional nativity so the children can see the type of natural barn Mary would have given birth in," I say. He shovels more food into his mouth and chews and I wait patiently.

"I really like that idea," he says.

"Thank you again for letting us have it there," I say.

I put my fork down and stand up. I throw my arms around Joseph and my body tingles. Shit, what am I doing?

"You're welcome," he whispers. It feels like everything has paused and our faces meet. Our noses brush and I feel the coldness of his against mine. I smile as he leans down and kisses me. My arms find his hair and it's soft and clean.

I melt into his kiss and it's softer and longer than last time. I enjoy the feel of his stubble against my face. I feel more alive than I ever did but will this mean something this time? When we pull away he looks intensely at me.

"I did want to apologies the other day for hurting you, it's been a while since I've spent an evening with anyone," Joseph says and I feel my heart thump. We sit back down again feeling awkward.

"It's okay," I say breathlessly. I am beyond happy. I want to ask what it means but would that scare him away? Should I just go with it?

I take a sip of my wine, wondering how the rest of the night will go.

"When we were on the sleigh I wanted to talk to you, I wanted to say I really hope you stay and I know what I said the other night but the girls really like you," Joseph says.

"I really like them, Joseph I still don't know what to do about staying though. What will I do after

Christmas? What if something happened between us and it didn't work? I've been hurt this month already," I say and look at him.

"Mum has been talking to me about you staying. I told her I don't want you to leave," he says.

"That first night I came to yours and you told me you basically drink by yourself every night. You are such a good person, you deserve the best," I say. He brings his chair around to my side.

"I've been on my own for three years now, I don't think I know how to be with anyone else," he says to me.

"I understand," I whisper. He strokes my cheek and my heart thumps. Do I have the courage to ask him this time? It's now or never. "If you want, we can go to my room," I whisper and he takes my hand.

CHAPTER 13

My eyes open and not to Ivy coming into my room this time. I can't believe I slept with Joseph. We weren't supposed to sleep together. Will this ruin our friendship now? Will everything be awkward? I look across and the sheets on his side of the bed are crumpled and empty. My heart sinks a little that he didn't stay.

I get myself up and showered and ready to go to school. Oh god, what do I tell Melanie and Angel?

Do I walk to school? It's only seven am and it's still dark outside. The street lamps are casting spotlights on the shadowy streets. I know it's a safe village but should I ask for a lift? My mind goes to Joseph. I can't ask him there's clearly a reason he left. What if he regrets what we did? I can't believe we slept together.

I shake off thoughts of Joseph as I walk out of the hotel and into the square. Most of the shops are setting off up for the morning. I wave to them as I walk past and head for the bakery.

"Hi Angel," I say. She looks knackered. "Do you

need help?"

"Yes please, oh could you take Jude to school this morning please? I have a huge order for the farm this afternoon, I don't know if anyone has said anything but Santa's grotto is opening after lunch for the children at the school so they are shutting early, every parent and child requires a mince pie," she says and points to the trays of mince pies in different stages of being baked.

"That's exciting," I say. I smile and take a finished mince pie.

"What the fuck happened to you?" she demands. She pulls the shutter down on the bakery and stands in front of me with her hands on her waist.

"Nothing," I say but I can tell my face is giving me away.

"OMG something happened," she whispers and I see a shadow at the blinds.

"Looks like you have a customer," I say, changing the subject.

Ivy smiles at both of us.

"Ah, Holly are you ready to go in?" Ivy asks.

"Yes I am, can Jude come with us?" I ask. Jude comes running down the stairs.

"Mummy, I can't find Spiderman," Jude wails. It takes a lot of bribery and tears to get him strapped in.

"Jude would you like to watch something?" I ask giving him my phone.

"Spiderman," he says and I figure out how to do it. Annoying theme songs blare out of my phone but at least Jude is silently watching. I get in next to Ivy.

"Thank you, Ivy, for the lift," I say.

"Well lovey, I did look to see if you were in your room but you had already got up. I wanted to talk to you about the noise coming from your room last night," she says casually.

Oh god. I cover my face and stare out of the window. She knows and I don't know what to say to her.

"Urm," I say. What do you say to the mum of the person you had sex with?

"I know it's none of my business but I just don't want either of you to get hurt," Ivy says. "I like you, Holly."

I smile at her. "I really like this village," I say.

"Then you know what to do, don't you?" she says.

The coach takes all of the children to the farm where the parents are waiting. We exit off the coach and the children run to their parents. I see Joseph and my stomach ties itself in knots. Oh god, what do we say to each other?

"Hi," he says casually.

"Hi," I say back. Seren and Star go to their dad and he picks them both up.

"Are you ready to see Santa?" he asks them. They cheer loudly and wriggle to be put down.

"What about you?" he asks me.

"What about me?" I repeat to him. The air between us feels so awkward. What do I say to him? Do I ask if that was a one-time thing? Has he forgotten the reason he didn't want a relationship? And what about me? I will be leaving soon, or I'm supposed to at least. It's now the seventh of December and I told Jake and Carol that I will be home by Boxing Day. It's a hard decision because this village is amazing but how can it be real? Once Christmas is done what am I supposed to do? What if I get hurt ? I can't take that again. Luke broke my heart.

"Will you be seeing Santa?" he asks me with a coy smile.

"Holly, how will Santa know what you want if you don't see him?" Seren asks. Her eyes are so sparkly with excitement I can't help but laugh.

"Okay, I will go and see Santa," I say. I follow the three of them, aware of how it must look to the gossiping mums. I bite my lip when I see Angel's stall set out with the rest of the market in a line outside of the barn. Everywhere is decorated in tinsel and lights. Gobble Di Gook is bobbing around looking for crumbs at the food stalls.

Angel sees me and mutters something. I pretend not to have seen her and just focus on the queue outside of the barn.

"Wow," I say to the three of them.

"We do Christmas properly here," Joseph says.

"I love Christmas," Star says.

"Me too," Seren adds. I smile at them and at Joseph. He's watching me and I feel nervous. What the fuck is he thinking?

"So do I," I say loudly and a few parents turn to us. "Christmas when I was at home used to be one of my favourite times of the year but then someone hurt me, someone I love," I say. I don't know why I'm telling the girls this.

"Did someone die?" Seren asks.

"Our mummy died," Star says. I swallow the lump and look up at Joseph who is biting his lip. He's probably wondering what I'm going to say.

"I bet your mummy is so proud of you and your daddy, she will be smiling down at you both," I say. Joseph beams at me and the girls cuddle close to my leg. I have to quickly wipe a tear from my face.

"Granny, can we see Santa now?" the girls ask when Ivy comes over to us.

"We have to be patient girls, Santa will be here all

day. Now what about you two?" she asks, glancing between me and Joseph.

"What about us Mum?" Joseph asks.

"It's nothing to do with me what you do, you're adults, but remember the girls need stability in their lives," she says to Joseph.

Joseph mumbles and Ivy takes the girls inside. We hadn't even realised the queue had moved.

"Mum's right," Joseph says and I nod, though I feel ridiculous.

"I wouldn't hurt you or the girls," I say in a whisper.

"I know, but you didn't say that you were staying either," Joseph says. I feel the tears and swallow desperately to get rid of them.

"I don't know if I can," I say.

"That's why I can't do a relationship," he says. He strokes my cheek and I nod. I really feel stupid now.

"I understand," I say.

"But I can do casual," he adds.

I look up at him wondering what he means. Casual as in just dates? Just sex?

"What?" I ask.

"I can do casual, no feelings, no messy business just..." he says trying to find the right words.

"Friends with benefits?" I ask. I look into his eyes to

see if he is joking and I can see he isn't. This doesn't sound like him at all.

"But, what about the girls?" I say.

"You don't need to worry about them personally," he says.

I have never been stunned into silence before but I am now. Joseph asking me not to care about the girls but then inviting me to see Santa with them. I'm so confused.

"Come in, the girls are waiting for you," Ivy says and Joseph goes to them. Ivy beckons me too and I follow.

"What did you ask Santa for?" Joseph asks.

"I can't tell you," Seren says.

"I want a mummy," Star says looking up at Joseph. Joseph looks like he is trying to keep his composure but I see the tears.

"Why don't we go for mince pies?" I say, trying to lighten the mood. The girls dance around us as we walk out the other side of the barn to the smell of food cooking. There are all different kinds of foods: chicken, candy floss and doughnuts, mince pies. Everyone has set up a market stall. I look around them and soak in the atmosphere. Someone is playing Christmas music nearby. This could be perfect place to sell my designs.

"So girls, what would you like to eat?" Joseph asks them when we walk back along the market stalls.

"Candy floss," they say together.

"Are you hungry?" he asks me. He envelopes my hand in his and it feels weird to be holding his hand. He doesn't want a relationship but he wants this? Is it just the feelings and emotions he doesn't want?

"No," I say. We sit at one of the picnic tables in the farm, Joseph and the girls one side and me on the other.

"Daddy, I've had fun today," Seren says.

"Can we invite Holly for more of our fun days?" Star asks.

"What do you think?" He looks at me for the answer.

"I would love to," I say and smile.

I feel the warmth again as I realise how much I will miss this little village. Pain stabs my heart a little as I think about it.

CHAPTER 14

Friday night drinks turned into inviting Joseph back to my hotel room, and now it's Saturday morning, the sheets are crumpled, and Joseph's gone. Today my stomach feels twisty and I feel like I need to talk to Angel or Melanie but then I wouldn't want to tell everyone his business. I know he is private but all my thoughts and feelings are sloshing around like a washing machine. This is more headache- inducing than a break up.

I take the fabric I bought from the market on Tuesday and the sewing machine Ivy lent me and get to work making costumes. I manage by five pm to make half of the costumes and when I hang them up and admire them I realise they actually look really good. This could be the first step towards getting my designs out there for the world to see.

A knock interrupts me half an hour later.

"Hello?" I hear outside the door.

"Oh. Hello there girls, Holly is working on school

costumes at the minute," Ivy says.

I turn off the sewing machine as I finish stitching and turn my design the right way around. The king's costume is made with a silver shiny waistcoat and golden trousers. I can't wait until our dress rehearsal this week before our final show next Friday.

"You can come in," I say and the door flings open. Ivy, Melanie and Angel are all standing outside.

"Can we see?" Ivy asks and I nod showing them my hung up designs. They sift through them, touching the fabric carefully and making comments.

"Holly these are amazing," Ivy says her eyes lighting up.

"So this is your secret talent then?" Melanie says. I might have mentioned designing a couple of times.

"Yes, I have dreamt of making clothes my entire life," I say to them. "I started with dolls clothes and I've even designed Christmas jumpers."

"Do you think you could have a couple of designs by Tuesday?" Ivy asks. I nod. "I might have a business opportunity for you."

I look at Melanie and Angel who beam at me proudly.

"To Christmas dreams coming true," Melanie says and we raise our shot glasses.

We repeat what she says and neck the shot.

"Oh god," I say when the liquid burns my throat. The pub is quite empty tonight but we decided after Ivy's little chat to come here and celebrate.

"My ex has Jude so it's nice to have child free time with the girls," Angel says.

"A-fucking-men." Melanie holds her glass up to toast.

"So how are you both still single?" I ask them.

"Because we don't want the drama of men," Angel says.

"Not at all?" I ask.

"What about your man, did you talk to him and tell him you like him?" Melanie asks.

"What, Joseph? Did I miss something?" Angel asks.

"Yes, you should have seen them last week, the chemistry was amazing," Melanie says and I blush.

"You like him, I knew you did," Angel says. They both stare at me with wide eyes.

"I'm so embarrassed," I moan and they look at each other.

"Why?" Melanie asks.

I sigh and put my head in my hands.

"I haven't told you what's been happening because

I don't really understand it myself," I say.

"You can't leave us in suspense," Melanie says.

"We wouldn't tell a soul," Angel says making a zip motion across her lips.

"Okay, we've slept together, twice," I whisper and they squeal. I shush them as a few villagers turn around to look at us.

"How? When?" Melanie starts bursting out with questions. "I only told you to tell him how you feel."

"I know, but then we started talking about only doing casual..." I trail off.

"So is it just sex?" Angel asks.

"God I wish I could find someone that just wanted that," Melanie says. I laugh.

"Believe me, you don't," I say.

"Is it just sex for both of you though?" Angel asks.

"Yes," I say.

"It never works," Melanie says.

"It will work," I say. "We both want that."

"I don't believe that after you telling me you like him," Angel says.

"Isn't it better than nothing?" I say, looking from one of them to the other.

"Not if feelings are there, you'll get hurt," Melanie says.

"I will be leaving in just over two weeks, there's no point getting into a relationship right?" I say looking at both of them. They look at each other.

"Are you still leaving then?" Melanie asks.

"I would have thought with what Ivy said you'd want to stay a bit longer," Angel says.

"Well, I suppose so, but what can she possibly do for me?" I ask. I fiddle with my hands because I'm nervous.

"I don't know, but if you want one of us to be there we can," Angel says.

"Of course," Melanie says.

"You know I want to get my designs out there but is it as simple as leaving my life behind for this one?" I say.

I've been pondering this. Can I leave my life? What about my friends and my parents? I feel like Tom Hanks in Splash.

"Are you happier here?" Angel asks.

"Yes," I answer instantly. "I've never been happier."

"You need to stop fighting it. We all moved here to get away from something we all took the plunge and it worked out," Melanie says.

"There's always a reason for everything you know. You found this village, surely that means something," Angel says.

"Well, I was crying because my boyfriend was in

bed with my boss and I got sacked, I missed my turning and followed the road to here," I say.

Is this it? Was I destined to come to this village and live my dream and meet a man I like who wouldn't ever cheat on me?

"There you go then," Angel says.

"You were supposed to meet us and Joseph and hey, maybe your dreams will come true on Tuesday," Melanie says.

CHAPTER 15

It's Tuesday and my stomach is in knots. I feel sick. Ivy has set up a meeting at the workshop and I'm wondering what it could possibly mean.

First though, I have to get through our dress rehearsal. I help the class change into their costumes and am delighted when they look amazing in them. It feels like my dream is already becoming a reality. When I go home, if I go home, maybe I can continue designing.

It's always been a definite that I will be going home but this morning I woke up with the possibility I could stay here for good.

I walk holding hands with Buddy and Noah, two little boys in Melanie's class. We walk into the hall of the school. They're wearing their innkeeper and shepherd costumes. We arrange them on the stage and Melanie goes to the piano to sort the music out.

The two narrators, Olwen and Angelica, come to the front. I have made them special outfits so they aren't left out.

They start off narrating and then the other two come up to join them. I put the map on the overhead projector and they carry on delivering their lines.

Melanie plays the intro to 'Little Donkey' with the words on the screen and I sing along with them. Melanie says I can and I want to. I want the children to have confidence in themselves. They've all worked so hard for this and I can't wait until Friday the last day of term, to perform in front of the entire school at the farm.

Things between Joseph and me are still strange. He keeps making physical contact with me and we kiss and I love it but he is still pulling away and when he mentions me leaving I just can't look him in the eyes. I'm terrified it will hurt him if I do leave but if I stay will I regret it in a few years?

I smile as the donkey and Mary and Joseph journey to Bethlehem. Townspeople are inside little wooden set houses that we had to paint after class.

"No room here," Eve says.

"You can come in here," Arthur says. Mary and Joseph look to me. I want to giggle because it's so adorable but I correct the line and we carry on. Melanie holds her thumbs up at all of us and I can't believe we've managed to do this in about two weeks. From just casting to us doing dress rehearsal. It's been chaotic but when the parents come to watch on Friday I hope I don't cry.

After we have finished, we sing 'Silent Night' together with the words up on the board. Then the cast take a bow and we all clap.

"That was amazing," I gush to them. Mr Tree stands at the door clapping.

"Well, Class One, that was fantastic," he says. I spin to face him and beam. I can't believe he was watching us this whole time.

"They've been practicing all week," Melanie says to Mr Tree.

"And you all absolutely look the part," he says and turns to me. "You made those?"

"Yes," I say and blush deeply. I don't know why Mr Tree makes me so nervous. Maybe because he is the head teacher. He seems proud of us and I should be beaming. Of course we are bloody good, we worked hard.

"Well, Class One I will look forward to seeing you all performing on Friday at the farm," he says.

"Can I borrow you Holly?" he asks. I look to Melanie who has now lined the class up to go back and nod. He takes me through to the staff room.

"So, Holly, I know this is unprofessional of me. I want to thank you for your hard work. But I've heard through the grapevine that you are leaving?" he asks.

"Boxing Day," I say. I swallow the lump in my throat. I'm still battling with myself over leaving. I don't want to have the argument with myself everyday while I'm still here.

"That's sad because I would have liked to offer you the chance to carry on working with the children. Your ideas have been fresh and the children really seem to enjoy your company. I know you aren't qualified but we can offer that," Mr Tree says.

I swallow down the lump again. I can't believe this village. It feels like wherever I've turned I am being offered opportunities. I've never been offered anything in my whole life. It feels way too good to be true.

"Urm, Mr Tree thank you so much for this opportunity," I say, the words racing out of my mouth.

"Look, I understand you have a meeting very soon for Ivy and Nick but I thought I would give you an alternative," he says.

"Thank you, can I think about it?" I ask.

"Of course," he says.

I walk back to the village and pace outside the workshop. I'm holding my portfolio and a couple of bags of my designs. Gobble Di Gook is watching me with his beady eyes. What is it with this turkey being everywhere?

The turkey makes me more nervous. I can't help thinking about this meeting. What if Ivy and Nick hate my designs? Will I be banished from the village? At least then I won't feel terrible about leaving. I can't get rid of the niggling feeling about leaving. When I mention it to anyone that feeling bubbles and gets worse. Do I give up and just stay? Should I leave earlier? Ivy told me to come by after school so they are expecting me. I feel physically sick.

"Come in darling," I hear from outside and I really think I'm going to throw up. My head starts spinning. This is the most scared I've ever been in my life.

I walk into the wooden workshop and stare in delight and surprise. It's absolutely amazing. It's like a little Santa's workshop with Nick in his costume obviously just finished being Santa at the farm for the day. There's people all over painting, designing and building what looks like beautiful wooden toys. I see a beautiful rag doll with brown hair wearing a pink dress. *I could design her clothes.* I think.

"Come through here." Ivy leads me to a small boxed room. She is wearing an apron covered in paint and has paint smudges on her cheeks too.

"This is incredible." I sigh and smile. I can't believe I've never been around here. No one really talks about the workshop but it's like an enormous factory. It's basically like Santa's workshop, if he was real of course.

"Holly, I see that you have a portfolio, can I see?" Ivy asks and I pass over my folder full of designs and little drapes of fabric. I bite my lip watching for her reaction. My stomach feels like a gymnastic doing flips and spins.

"I didn't have time to put lots together but that is basically what I do. I've done fancy dress and I brought the Mary costume for you to see," I say and hand it to her. She feels the fabric and shakes it out so it's all straight.

"You really have an incredible talent," she says.

"I've been doing this as a hobby for so many years, I did a degree at college but then had to find a job quickly so I never pursued it," I say.

"Shall we get down to it?" Ivy asks and I nod. I feel like all of the spit has left my mouth and it's so dry. I physically feel sick and my hands are shaking. I can't believe I'm here.

"Have you visited the toy shop next to the workshop yet?" she asks.

"Yes very briefly, but I've been so busy," I say. I feel a little disappointed that I might have ruined my chances now by not studying the merchandise.

"When we finish I want to take you in there, we've been designing new dolls this year and predict they will sell amazingly. They are called the Fruity Tooties. The reason they are called that because each doll is a different fruit so we have a strawberry doll, an orange doll, do you get the idea?" she asks.

"Yes," I say and she carries on.

"We were looking to design outfits for these dolls and needed someone but we haven't been able to come up with anything yet. We've got the dolls all ready but they have no outfits on them. I know with school you are busy but if you can design something by, let's say Sunday? Then we will be able to release the dolls just in time for Christmas. Of course we would be paying you for your time and designs. If they sell amazingly you would get a share in the profits and if everything goes to plan we would like to bring you to work in our workshop as a designer. We have three designers here already but we think your skills would fit in brilliantly around here," she says.

My eyes fill with tears as I think about everything she has said. Should I take the plunge? It's everything I've ever wanted in my life. It could lead to being able to design adults clothes and maybe even opening my own shop.

"Ivy, thank you so much for the opportunity," I say. "Yes, I want to be involved."

"There's one catch though," she says. "You have to stay here after Christmas." I nod thinking it over.

"Can I get back to you tomorrow on that one?" I ask and she nods.

"Now, let me show you around the toyshop," she says. She gives me my portfolio back and I walk next to her obediently. My heart is pounding out of my chest. I've been given the one thing I've always wanted and all I have to do is stay. Why is it so hard to just say yes I will stay?

I need to pinch myself and just say yes. I can't think of any reason to go home apart from my friends who I will be ringing later to talk to about this. Will they come to visit me if I stay? Of course they would.

We stop outside the red shop with rocking horses out front like a carousel house with a coin slot machine. I run my hands along the smoothness of the horse. It's absolutely beautiful I don't know how I didn't notice it before.

"I can see you have a good eye for toys," she says. "My husband personally carved this one."

"It's incredible," I say and smile.

We walk into the shop with shelves going all around. The till is right next to the doors and a smiling faces greets me.

"Hi Holly, welcome to Rudolph's Toy Shop" she says.

"Hello Ava," Ivy says.

"I hear you might be joining the crew, welcome

aboard," she says shaking my hand.

"Yes, we are very lucky that Holly found us," Ivy says. I wander around looking at all of the bears. They're all hand made by the workshop and I can tell that everything is made with love.

"Mum?" I hear the shop door open and Joseph suddenly appears wearing wellies, jeans and a hoodie. His wellies are covered in mud.

"Hello darling have you finally come to do your shopping for the girls?" ivy asks.

"Yes, I know I'm late but I have no idea what they want," Joseph asks.

"Did you ask them?" Ivy asks.

"Yes, they want dolls. You know they love their dolls," Joseph says. He sees me and his smile is hard to ignore. "Hi Holly," he says, and my heart races.

"I'm just giving Holly a tour of the shop. She is going to be helping with our new line of dolls."

"That's amazing, congratulations," Joseph says.

I feel pride building up inside me.

"I'll do it," I say. "I'll stay here."

"You're staying?" Joseph asks. I nod. Wondering if that means things will be different now.

Ivy hugs me. "I can't wait to see what you have in mind. Do you want to continue the tour with Joseph?" she asks.

"Yes," I say probably too quickly.

"I look forward to seeing you on Sunday," Ivy says and leaves.

I'm left with Joseph and I don't know what to say to him.

"I'm so thrilled you've decided to stay," Joseph says

"I can't wait to see what this village has in store for me," I say.

I smile. I never thought I would meet anyone else I liked after Luke hurt me but spending time with Joseph has been my favourite part of December. I also can't wait to see what happens with Ivy's dolls.

"Anything is possible in this village," he says.

"Well, I'm hoping I've nearly paid off my hotel room. I feel awful that I came here with no money."

I didn't think about my living arrangements before I arrived and here I am not really thinking about it again. Maybe I need to grow up and start thinking about my future.

 "Mum loves having you around but if you want to you can stay with me," he suggests and I look at him in surprise. I know we've been sleeping together well, twice now but how would that work?

"What about the girls?" I ask.

"The girls think the world of you. I wouldn't want

anyone else in their lives," he says.

"What are you saying?" I ask. He takes a step towards me and smiles.

"Do you want to upgrade our relationship?" he asks.

"What about all of the reasons you gave for why we couldn't be together?" I ask.

It feels weird that he's finally sharing the feelings I have for him but can I do this? Can we have a relationship?

"I'm willing to try again," he says. "I can't stay away from you."

I gulp and we share a kiss inside the toy shop. "I thought you were giving me a tour," I say.

He shows me around the toy shop and it's actually massive. It has an amazing section for Christmas toys that's full of Santas and angels. I help Joseph pick up a couple of dolls for Seren and Star and I pick up a doll to be our Jesus in the nativity. It's only three days until we are performing in front of everyone and I'm so excited. There's one thing I need to do though.

"How did you manage that then?" Carol asks when I ring her as soon as I'm back in the hotel room. I've ordered my lunch to the room and Ivy doesn't seem to mind.

"I was at the right place at the right time. It just felt right," I say.

"Look at you Mrs Drama Coach," Carol says though I know she's impressed.

"So, when is she going to invite us to the nativity?" I hear Jake ask in the background.

"You heard him," Carol says.

"Well, can you leave work to come?" I ask.

"Did you not tell her?" Jake asks.

"Tell me what?" I ask. I put the phone closer to my ear.

"Kelly has been fired and no one else has come in. The rest of the seasonal staff quit and it's just been us," Carol says.

"Oh," I say. "Is that what you wanted the other day?"

"We didn't want to disturb your holiday," she says.

"So what are you going to do?" I ask.

"We've quit too," Jake says. "We don't want to work at a company that treats our friend so badly."

"Oh guys, you didn't have to do that," I cry. I nearly do actually cry. I can't believe they've left. We'd all been there for so long.

"We will start looking after Christmas but we were hoping to come and see you, and now this nativity is the perfect excuse," Carol says.

"You'll just have to help us find it," Jake says.

"Oh yes, how come we couldn't see it on the map?" Carol asks.

I have no answer.

"Do you remember arriving?" Carol asks.

"No." I shake my head even though they can't see. "I'll talk to Ivy," I say.

"Okay. You know we love you don't you?" they shout down the phone.

"Of course," I say and we hang up.

It feels weird that my friends are going to see my new life. I wonder if I look any different in the mirror. Am I happier? I want to think that I can have something with Joseph and I don't' know why I'm holding back. I should just go for it and see what happens. Why not?

I text him to come around and wait until he does. He knocks lightly on the door.

"Come in," I say.

"I'm really pleased you text," he says coming straight up to me. It's always so weird how all I want to do is kiss him yet I'm holding back.

"I really want to give it a try," I say and we kiss before tumbling into bed.

CHAPTER 16

I'm beyond nervous, today is the day I bring Jake and Carol to meet Joseph and the children will perform their nativity.

"You need a good breakfast to keep you going today," Ivy says, presenting me with a fry up. Joseph has joined me for breakfast.

"I'm looking forward to seeing your friends," Joseph says, making conversation. He's offered to come and pick up Jake and Carol with me later, and although I'm excited, nerves swirl in my stomach too. I cut my bacon up and stuff it in my mouth.

"Me too, but it's weird, they said they couldn't find the place on the map," I say. It seems like the right time to bring this up.

"Oh yes, it isn't on the map. It's a magical village," Joseph says.

I look at him to see if he's joking but his face is serious. "Does that mean you can't ever leave once you're here?" I ask. Maybe it is like Splash.

"No not at all. But it's only there if you really see it," he says.

"I don't understand. How did I see it?" I ask.

"You were escaping a relationship," he says.

"So were you born in this village?" I ask.

"Yes, it was much smaller when I was a child. The school only had one class. Over the years more people like you have arrived and stayed," he says.

"I love that about the place. It's so inviting," I say with a smile.

"If you hadn't left your boyfriend we wouldn't have met." He reaches his hand out and takes mine. I squeeze his and he kisses my cheek. I can't believe the man that never dates is mine.

"That's true," I say, and smile.

"Daddy, Daddy it's time to go," Seren comes in and Joseph drops my hand. I frown. Has he told the girls about us?

"Come on then pumpkin," Joseph says.

"Daddy, I'm an angel," she says.

I follow them out of the hotel to where the tractor is. Star is already in it with Ivy next to her. I give Ivy a hug.

"Hello love," she says and I get in next to Joseph.

"Hi," I say.

"Granny are you coming to watch me?" Star asks.

"Of course I am," Ivy says.

"We will be heading to the barn about four," I say.

"Holly, I can't wait to sing with you," Seren says.

"Me too and you've both been practicing so hard," I say and smile. I catch Joseph's eye and feel nervous. What if we can never go back now? If we ruin our relationship can we still be friends? I still think about the way Joseph yanked his hand away when the girls saw us. Isn't being in a relationship supposed to be a thing you aren't embarrassed about?

"You will both be amazing," Joseph says.

We travel down the road bumpily on the tractor. I really need to get my own car fixed. The road is icy and the wind is a little strong. Luckily we've got hats, scarves and gloves.

When we park by the school we are early and it starts drizzling as we park up. I frown. It didn't say it was going to rain today.

"Have a good day girls," he says and hugs and kisses his daughters. I walk with them into the classroom. The girls follow me. It's only a couple of minutes before the bell.

"Morning Holly, all ready for tonight?" Melanie asks.

"Definitely," I say. "It's started raining," I add looking out of the window. It's coming down a little more now. "Fingers crossed the rain eases up." I cross my fingers like a child.

Melanie sits on her teacher chair as the kids come

in chatting and excited. It's also the last day of term before Christmas and Melanie has organized an exciting Santa visit in the school hall.

"Can everyone sit on the carpet please?" Melanie asks and I help all of the children sit down after putting their coats away. I hover next to them waiting until we start the class. Melanie takes the register and we all line up for assembly. I can't help feeling excited for the children.

"Come in children," Mr Tree says and stands by the door. The children sit in a semi-circle.

"Holly, have you thought about what I said?" Mr Tree asks.

I nod. "Yes, I want to thank you so much for this opportunity and I don't want to put all of my eggs into one basket yet but I've been offered an amazing opportunity by Ivy and Nick," I say

"I understand," he says and pats me on the shoulder. Other people would probably think it's patronising but I smile. He finally likes me.

"Ho, ho, ho!" A voice comes from the speaker and the children gasp and look around.

"Santa!" All the children shout and chant for Santa.

"Ho ho ho." The sound continues until Santa comes through the door. The screams are deafening. All of the children stand up and run to Santa.

"Hello boys and girls," he shouts in his gruff voice.

I smile as the children crowd him.

"Would you like to hear a story?" he asks.

"Yes," they shout. I grab a chair next to Melanie and we watch them.

"I tell you now I almost got lost on my journey to the school but can anyone guess which reindeer helped guide the way?" he asks.

All of the children's hands shoot up.

"Yes," Santa says, pointing at one of the boys.

"Rudolph," Jude says and I smile. He beams when Santa praises him.

"That's right. Rudolph is my extra special reindeer. Does anyone know a song about Rudolph?" Santa asks.

"Rudolph the Red-Nosed Reindeer," they all shout.

The class sings 'Rudolph the Red Nosed Reindeer' and then follow it with 'When Santa Got Stuck Up The Chimney'.

"Now, before I go," Santa says after the kids finish their songs. "I have special permission to give each of you a gift before Christmas. No it isn't a bottle of beer, I'm sorry," he says and we chuckle.

The kids line up and each receives their gifts. By the time we get them to their classroom there is a buzz in the air. I've never felt so Christmassy before in my life.

"That was adorable," I say to Melanie and follow

her outside. We are on playtime duty and I wrap up. The rain is still drizzling and it doesn't look like it's going to stop anytime soon.

"It was, we do that every year and it never gets old," Melanie says with a smile.

"So, how is everything with you?" she asks, looking at me. We walk around the perimeter of the playground while the children play. We are wrapped up in our coats, hats and scarves because the wind is so cold. The children don't seem to feel any of it. They have changed into their wellies and have their hats and gloves on. They're keeping warm by kicking around footballs and running after each other.

"Everything seems to be going really well," I say. "I still can't believe Ivy has given me a chance to make clothes for her new doll line. I'm really excited about it."

"I'm really pleased for you," she says.

"Thank you," I say.

"So are you still leaving?" she asks.

"No," I say.

"Have you told Joseph you're not leaving?" she asks.

"Yes, he seems happy I'm staying," I say.

I haven't really spoken to Joseph too much. I want to go out somewhere with him but he's been so busy with the girls that I haven't pushed it.

"Will you take your relationship to a new level?" she asks.

"He's asked me to but I'm still so confused about everything," I say.

"Why?" Melanie asks.

"Because he hasn't told the girls about us and everything still feels secretive. I don't want to be someone's dirty secret," I say.

"So are you just going to carry on sleeping together?" she asks.

"Yes, but I think we need another conversation about what we both want from this relationship," I say.

"I think that's a good idea," she says.

It's nice to have someone to talk to. It's nice to have friends and I can't wait to get to know them now that I'm staying here longer. I suddenly feel guilty that I won't be a teaching assistant with her anymore. Have I put all my eggs into one basket thinking that making dolls clothes will get me what I want?

"He said he would always put the girls first and I get that but I want someone that loves me. I know that's selfish and I would never ask him to choose me over the girls. I'm sick of being cheated on and being alone," I say.

Melanie blows the whistle before she can answer. I feel like I've poured my heart out and it felt good. Now I just need to tell the right person everything I've just told Melanie.

CHAPTER 17

J oseph is waiting by the school in an actual car. Wait. Is that my car? How did he get my car?

"Hi," I say with a smile.

"I fixed your car, I thought I would surprise you," he says. I smile as I take a look around it.

"It's perfect, thank you," I say.

"Another surprise," Joseph says. Jake and Carol step out of the car and I squeal as we all hug.

"I was supposed to come with you to get them," I say.

"I know, I wanted to surprise you," Joseph says and kisses me.

"Nice looking guy you got there," Jake whispers to me.

"Guys, we better get to the farm, the nativity starts soon," I say, glancing up at the sky and hoping it doesn't rain again.

We pile into the car and I drive. Joseph is next to me and I ignore the looks from Jake specifically.

"Can we have the radio on?" he whines.

"Fine," I say putting a random Christmas station on. Baby It's Cold Outside comes on and I smile and look over at Joseph. I wonder if he cherishes this song as much as I do.

"OMG, I love this song," Jake says and starts singing loudly.

"What do you think of them?" I say.

"They are very interesting, I can't wait to get to know them better," he whispers, and we giggle at them.

He puts his hand over mine and I feel the spark between us. I want to hold his hand but I'm aware of my friends near us. I want to have the conversation with him about where we are in our relationship, but I just can't bring myself to bring it up and definitely not with Carol and Jake in the back of the car.

I look up at him and smile and receive a beautiful smile back. My body has turned into a jelly mess. His smile is amazing.

I don't want him to think I've changed my mind. Why is this so confusing?

We arrive and park up on his drive. I can't believe my car is working now. The parking area is full and people are coming in all directions.

The front of the farm is crowded with customers at the line of stalls. Everyone in the village is so talented. Maybe next year it will be me on a stall selling my own designs.

I still need to get my head into Ivy's designed. I've put aside an entire day for my designs tomorrow and I can't wait. I've been thinking up ideas since Ivy asked me and I can't wait to share them with everyone.

"What a pretty village, no wonder you don't want to come home," Carol whispers. I laugh.

"You can't blame me," I say.

Jake links his arm through mine. "So, tell me what is going on with you and Joe?" he asks.

"I don't know what you mean," I say. They follow me towards the farm where Melanie is already waiting.

"You so do, don't think I didn't see you holding hands." He looks me up and down suspiciously.

"You got here, thank god. The kids are high on sugar and Christmas spirit and everyone is hyper," Melanie says looking stressed.

"I'm here now, I'm sorry, my friends have just arrived. Melanie this is Carol, Carol Melanie and Jake," I say. Everyone politely says hello and shakes hands. I am whisked by Melanie into Ivy and Nick's house where the children are getting ready. Ivy is helping with costumes and I start looking for missing items and helping children do up buttons.

I could do with a glass of something by the time we

are done.

"Children, we are starting in the little barn remember, and please keep the turkey in the barn," Melanie says aiming this one at Star and Seren who are holding half of Gobble Di Gook each. "Then you have to travel to Bethlehem. You go around the garden twice while singing. If anyone gets stuck I'm here and Miss Willows is here too."

"Miss, I can't find my star," Star says and I can see she's in tears. She lets the turkey go and he starts pecking the ground.

"I can't get my shoes on," Arthur says. Melanie goes to help Arthur while I follow Ivy looking for the star.

"We had it about ten minutes ago," she says.

"It can't have gone far," I say looking through the box.

One of the boys runs through the room and Star follows crying.

"He has my star," she yells. I take the star from the boy and give it to Star.

"Now, Alex, that wasn't nice was it? Imagine if someone took something you needed," I say.

"Sorry Miss Willows," he says. I let him go back and follow the kids to their bench.

I open the barn door a crack and see the rows of chairs with parents and family members. I spot

Joseph at the front with his mum and dad. Jake and Carol are sitting together behind Joseph.

"Is everyone ready?" I ask and I am met by nods and cheers.

"Narrators, can you come and stand here," I say and they follow me.

"Mary, Joseph and the angels you follow Miss Snowflake to the mini barn," I say and Melanie leads them out.

I open the doors and Angelica steps up to the front of the crowds and introduces the nativity.

The audience claps as the children go through their lines and I'm so proud that everyone is remembering them.

The donkey and horse get a laugh from the audience and I look at everyone wanting to savour this night. This must be what it feels like to accomplished something.

The children stand up and everyone sings 'Little Donkey'. Even the audience join in and I clap at the end of the song with everyone else and put my thumbs up encouragingly.

The narrators carry on and I go behind the scenes, setting up the little pop-up tent houses we use for inns.

"There's no room at the inn," Noah, Eva and Arthur say.

"But we have come so far," Noella says

"And my wife is having a baby," Rudy says.

I help the other children out of the barn as Mary and Joseph walk in with all of the real animals and children dressed as animals.

"It's not amazing," says Rudy.

"But it will do," Noella says.

The narrator continues and I join in with 'Away in A Manger' with the class. Noella is cuddling the doll used as the baby Jesus to her chest and I smile at her. The audience are also smiling and waving to their children. We've successfully pulled off a nativity in the barn and nothing has gone wrong. I'm actually amazed that even the rain managed to die down to just a bit of spitting by the time we had started.

The narrator continues on and we get to the shepherds who, with Joseph's help, are in the other barn with the sheep.

I quickly give them masks as they discuss leaving the sheep.

"Hey I'm not missing out," Elliot shouts.

"He isn't responsible enough anyway, he would lose the sheep," Buddy says.

I get the children ready to sing The First Noel' and we all stand up to sing. I catch Joseph's eye and see his eyes twinkle. My heart skips a beat and I have to look away.

Star stands up and starts doing ballet dance moves. I smile at her and everyone starts aahing as the wise men follow Star around the ground and straight to Mary and Joseph.

"We bring you gifts of gold, frankincense and myrrh," they say, and then they leave.

Everyone stands up and they all sing 'Silent Night' and then the audience erupt into a standing ovation.

"Class One that was absolutely brilliant, I think all of the parents will agree with me. I would like to thank Mrs Snowflake and Miss Willows. Let's give them another round of applause," Mr Tree says and the crowd erupt into clapping.

I feel a little tearful as I hug Melanie and the children in a huge class hug. I will miss the kids. Even though I'm staying it won't be the same as it was. I feel that lump rising. I can't design clothes and work with the children. I would be happy to work with the school again. A girl can't have too many skills now.

"That was incredible girls," Joseph says and I smile as I help them into their coats and take them to their dad.

"Thank you," Joseph says.

"Thank you Holly," Seren says and they both hug me.

"We don't want you to leave the school," Star says.

"You're leaving the school?" Joseph asks with his eyebrow raised.

"I can't design doll clothes and work at the school," I say.

"So you haven't changed your mind?" he asks.

"No," I say with so much certainty I seem desperate.

He takes a step closer to me and I feel his arms around mine. If this is the welcome I get for staying, bring it on.

CHAPTER 18

"**W**ake up bitch," Jake shouts as he hammers on my door. I sit up feeling groggy. After the nativity we all went to the pub and had a party. We drank way too much and had too much fun but it was nice introducing my new friends to my old friends.

"I'm awake," I shout. Today is supposed to be spent making designs for the dolls for my pitch tomorrow but now Jake and Carol are here I guess I should show them around. I've got time to do both and it's not a big deal.

"Can I come in? You haven't snuck the dishy farmer in here have you?" Jake asks. Ha, as if. I really wanted to go back with him last night but I couldn't leave my friends on their own.

"Yes, I saw you and Joseph you know. You might think it's subtle but my love radar was off the charts," he says, tapping his nose.

"Morning, can I borrow your loo?" Carol comes in and I've seen ghosts that look better than she does.

"Of course," I say gesturing towards the door. "I

will admit there is something there."

"I knew it," Jake says.

"But his girls will always be first, so I'm not sure I'll ever be that important to him,'" I say and I know it sounds awful but I still feel sad about it.

"Are you okay Caz?" I call, when she doesn't reappear from the bathroom. I look back to Jake who raises his eyebrow at me.

"Have you gone all serious on us or something? You seem different," Jake says.

"I'm happy here," I say "I feel like I've found my place. I've been offered to showcase my designs," I say.

It's really weird that usually these two know everything about my life but I've been so busy I haven't been able to tell them everything that's been going on. It almost feels like this was all a dream bubble and they have come to join it and now I'm wondering is it all a dream? Will Ivy really want me designing clothes for the dolls?

"Holz that's amazing, you are super- duper talented," Jake says and hugs me. I hug him.

"So you are definitely staying here?" he asks.

"Yes, and not just for Christmas," I say.

"What's going on with you and farmer boy then?" he asks.

"It's complicated," I say.

He rolls his eyes at me. He hates that word.

"It really isn't," he says.

"He's right." Carol comes back looking a little better.

"Are you feeling okay?" I ask her.

"Yes, you know I'm not used to getting drunk. It always knocks me back. I agree though, it isn't complicated," Carol says.

"What do I tell him is the reason I have come to see him though?" I ask. Carol and Jake have ransacked my clothes and I have refused to wear their very short 'more like a nightie than a dress. "This isn't a good idea," I say. I just want to concentrate on my pitch for tomorrow.

"Of course it is," Jake says and he shoves me out of the door. I take my bag and walk the few minutes to the farm.

I will never stop being amazed at the view from the top of the hill of the square and surrounding fields. The fluffy white sky stretches across the entire field. The rain from yesterday has stopped but the ground is still wet.

I pause outside the door. Will he even be in? Could he be somewhere with the girls today? I see him in the distance in one of the fields and smile. He is on his own so I wonder where the girls are.

I casually walk to the field and see him with the animals. He looks so natural with them and so gentle. I could watch him all day.

He doesn't notice me at first and I happily watch him pouring food into troughs. He looks up and sees me. Our eyes connect and I feel the butterflies.

"Hi," I say at the gate.

He opens it and lets me in. "Did you ever meet Kenny and Dolly?" he asks and points to the sheep.

"No," I say.

"Well, you know the song islands in the stream? Well the sheep are named after Kenny Rogers and Dolly Parton, it's my mum and dad's favourite song," he says.

"Wow," I say.

"So anyway, I'm waffling on and I haven't asked if you'd like a coffee at the house?" he says.

"Yes please," I say with a smile. I will get around to finishing my designs. It means more than anything to me. I actually carry them around with me in a little diary in my bag.

We reach the house and he opens the door for me. Hopefully this time my visit won't end in tears.

"Do you want tea, coffee, water?" he asks.

"Coffee is fine," I say. "Where are the girls?" I ask.

"They are at Angels for a play date with Jude," he says.

"Ah okay, that sounds like fun. I'm going to miss that class," I say and sigh. Joseph puts the hot coffee in front of me.

"My mum has been talking about your designs for the last few days you know," he says and sits opposite me.

"I'm so nervous," I say.

"So have you done them already?" he asks.

"Sort of, I've done the designs for a couple of them but I need to finish them off."

"Can I see?" he asks. Usually I go really shy and don't like showing off my designs but it feels different with Joseph. He's seen me naked and for some reason it doesn't seem as scary showing them to him.

I take the notebook out of my bag, full of colourful designs and bits of fabric stuck on everywhere.

"These are unique," he says and looks up at me smiling.

"I really hope your mum likes them," I say.

"She will love them. I love them and I'm the wrong demographic for them. The girls would definitely love them," he says.

"Speaking of the girls, I mostly came today for two reasons, one is to ask what they want for Christmas and, well.." I stop and feel suddenly awkward. He looks at me expectantly. What do I say?

"You could make them something for Christmas?" he says. "They have a dolls house but we haven't done much with it. It has furniture but the dolls are a little rubbish," he says. He shows me and they are mostly bottle corks with faces drawn onto them. I smile because it's so cute that he has done that for them. They really are so lucky to have him.

"What about the second reason?" he asks. He sits next to me in his jeans, smelling like citrus. I wrap my fingers around my cup looking up at him.

"Joseph, I want us to be together. I want everything and I don't care how selfish that sounds, and I want the girls and everyone to know. I don't want to be a dirty little secret away from your family."

I bite my lip anxiously waiting for his reaction. He leans over and takes my hand.

"Forgive me, Holly I am new to all of this and I've not had a relationship since the girls mum. I'm sorry I made you feel like you were a dirty secret, that was never my intentions. I feel like the luckiest man in the world to be given another chance at finding someone and I am so proud of you, I would never hide you away," he says, whispering the last part.

Our faces move closer to each other and our lips touch. When we pull away I feel like it's my turn to say something, though I'm breathless.

"I feel the same way," I say. "I'm so lucky to have found you when I needed someone the most but I worry about the girls. You said you can't do a relationship because of them but I don't want you keeping secrets from them."

"I promise we won't keep it from them. So do you want to make this official?" he asks

"Yes," I answer simply.

"The girls absolutely adore you," Joseph says.

"I love them too. I never really thought of kids before but seeing them with you and being a part of it it just makes me feel happy," I say.

"I can't think of anyone better suited to them than you," he says.

"Really?" I ask feeling caught off guard. He catches my tone.

"Of course, that's if you want the responsibility," he says.

"I can't think of anything else I want more," I say.

He pulls me into a kiss again and I feel like the luckiest girl in the world. I have a boyfriend and I get to be involved in the lives of the two little girls who I adore.

"Now can you help me get my pitch together?" I ask.

CHAPTER 19

I can't stop smiling as I get out of the shower at Joseph's and into my confident pitch clothing. A grey skirt, light blue blouse and grey blazer. I pace outside the workshop again feeling déjà vu from Tuesday. I can't believe I've been given this opportunity. It's weird how something that went so wrong can have led to everything going so right. If I hadn't caught Luke with Kelly I would still be with the bastard and I'd have never met any of the amazing people in this village. I wouldn't have been given this opportunity to pitch my dolls' clothing.

I'm still a little early so I sit on the bench outside and go over my notes. I've rehearsed in front of Joseph and although it felt really weird he was supportive and asked me questions that made me think of other ideas. Overall I think I did well. Now though I feel like all the moisture from my mouth has gone and I'm not sure I'll be able to talk. My minds gone blank and I'm worried I'll forget everything. Oh god, what if I forget everything?

"Hello Holly love." Ivy comes outside with her

warm blue eyes and bright smile. Usually her appearance makes me feel better but today I feel the opposite. I feel like I might throw up at any moment. She has given this task to me and I actually can't believe it.

I follow her through into a little quiet room with two sofas. "Would you like a drink love? Tea? Coffee?" she asks.

"Water please," I say when I find my voice. I'm worried anything else will make me bring it back up.

She comes back with Nick and a glass of water for me.

"Hello my love, I'm sorry we haven't really had a chance to get to know each other properly," he says and I shake hands with him. He looks so much like Joseph but a little older. I see the love between them when they sit down together on the sofa and smile at each other. This is what I want. I want someone to look at me like that.

"So, Holly, I'm really excited to see what you have come up with," Ivy says and I stand up. I bring my notebook out of my bag and open it up to the dolls. Ivy sent me an email with the dolls so I know what they look like. Each of them is a different colour and fruit and they smell vaguely of the fruit they look like.

"So, the ones I particularly want to show you today are the orange and strawberry. I know it might look bulky but this is my idea for the orange doll."

I take out the outfit I put together to show them. It's a dress that's very orange with ballet skirt ruffles on it. The top is shaped like an orange segment. Ivy's face lights up and Nick looks interested too.

"The strawberry is the same, ruffled red skirt and the top part is a strawberry with the little seeds inside it. The outfits can come off and obviously be mixed and matched so the strawberry top can easily go with the orange skirt. I can do more too for any other fruit in any other colour," I say.

I show Ivy the fabric designs that Joseph helped me with. He is very good at designs and he told me that's because of the girls.

"We are going to have a discussion, there are biscuits in the kitchen and if you do want a hot drink help yourself," Ivy says.

They leave the room and I pace. I can't make a drink. I'm shaking so badly. I wish Joseph was with me to make me feel better.

I finish the water and clean the glass. I look out of the window at the farm and it looks so peaceful. It almost makes me feel better.

Ivy and Nick come back in with the two girls.

"Hi girls." I smile at them and they hug me.

"We will miss you, Holly," they say. "Can't you be our teacher please, please," Seren asks.

I look at them both confused. Have they been talking about me?

"Now, girls, we have spoken about this. It is Holly's decision what she wants to do," Ivy says. "So Holly back to what we were talking about. We have had a conversation with the girls as well, seeing as they are the target audience for the dolls. Girls, what do you think to these dresses for Granny and Grandpa's designs?" Ivy asks them

"I really like them Granny," Seren says.

"Me too," Star adds. I smile. Surely they are just biased towards me because they like me but I appreciate it.

"We would like to get you involved in the workshop Holly. We know we don't have long to get these dolls out before Christmas, we started all of this pretty late in the year so we would like to get these dresses into production immediately." I struggle to focus on the words coming out of her mouth "Holly, we are offering you the position of fabric designer for the workshop. For whenever we make dolls or anything that needs clothes or furniture making for it," Ivy says.

I look at both of them and almost feel like I'm going to have a heart attack.

"Are you serious?" I ask.

"Very serious. Can you start Tuesday morning?" she asks.

I nod because I'm not sure what to say. I'm absolutely thrilled. It's everything I've ever wanted.

"On Tuesday morning I will take you for a tour around the workshop and we will start the designs on the dolls. We've been looking for someone like you for a while," Nick says. We shake hands.

Ivy hugs me. "Welcome to the family," she says and squeezes me. I wonder if she means the workshop or her actual family.

I walk out of the workshop excited.

I can't believe I've been given the opportunity to follow my dream. It all might actually come true for me.

I stand on the hill next to the farm and look over towards the square. I wonder what everyone is doing right now. Should I go back down the hill and tell everyone I got the job or shall I just stay here and soak up the moment? I want to tell Joseph more than anyone even though I think he might already know. The girls come out of the workshop and see me.

"Holly," Seren says and they run up to me. I'm immediately circled and squeezed to death.

"Can you make me a Christmas dress for the party?" she asks.

"Can you make my dolls clothes for her?" Star asks.

"Now girls, that isn't fair. Let Holly take in this big

opportunity," Joseph says and smiles.

"News travels fast," I say and smile. I look at the girls.

"I would love to make you clothes if I have time. Maybe I can have a word with Santa about your presents," I say.

"Yes please," Star says.

"I didn't ask Santa for dolls' clothes," Seren says.

"Oh," I say and look at Joseph who looks confused

"What did you ask for baby?" he asks.

"A new mummy," she whispers.

I suck in my breath, looking up at Joseph who wraps his arms around her.

"Oh princess," he says and I see a tear in his eye. This feels like a much too personal moment for me to be here for.

"I'm sorry Daddy but I miss Mummy," Star says.

"Don't ever be sorry," Joseph says and picks her up. "I'm sorry about this," he says to me.

"Don't be," I say with a sad smile. I gulp down the lump in my throat.

"Come back to the house with us," Joseph says and I nod. I like that he includes me in the invitation even though the conversation is very personal and nothing to do with me.

"Can I show you my dolls?" Star asks.

"Of course," I say

"Yay," they scream and run ahead. We catch up with them and walk into the cottage. Joseph puts the kettle on to make drinks.

"Holly, we want you come up to our room," Seren says.

"Please say yes," Star adds.

I look to Joseph who shrugs.

"Of course," I say and they pull me upstairs with them. I open their door and there are toys everywhere. The girls' beds have canopies hanging over them. A massive dolls' house is in the middle of the floor. I hear footsteps and Joseph comes up with a tray.

"Please be careful with the drinks girls," Joseph says. "You too," he whispers and kisses my cheek.

I smile. "Thank you,"

"So this is my bed, Holly," Seren says and shows me her teddies. "This is Elsa and this is Mr Paws." She shows me them and I hold out my hand and shake their little hands.

"They are beautiful," I say.

"My mummy made the dress for my bear," Seren says.

"Did she?" I ask.

She nods. "Mummy used to sew me lots of dresses and for my teddies."

"That's amazing," I say and look at the dress she is wearing. It's a t shirt dress with flowers and plaid patterns on it.

"I didn't know your wife made clothes," I say to Joseph when the girls are busy playing.

"Yes, she was always at the sewing machine. When I found out you made clothes it was an amazing coincidence," Joseph says. I take my cup, feeling uncomfortable. Is that why he liked me? Because I reminded him of his wife? Is that why the girls wanted me around?

"That's really interesting," I say to the girls who show me the dolls' house their dad made them. He's made bottle cork characters of the girls with their actual faces stuck to them.

"Daddy says we can have some toys for the house for Christmas. And Santa said he would see," Star says.

"Well it's worth asking, isn't it?" I say. The girls looked so hopeful when I said I might be able to make them some clothes I couldn't have said no.

"Of course it is. Did you ask Santa for that?" Joseph asks.

"Yes," Star says.

"No I still want a mummy," Seren says.

"I know angel," Joseph says and she climbs on to his lap.

"Can Holly stay for a sleepover?" Star asks.

I look at Joseph and he looks at me. Will the girls start asking questions about us? Did he tell them about us being in a relationship?

"Urm," Joseph says.

"Please Daddy," Star says. She starts doing a really cute look with her hands praying. Joseph looks at me as if to ask if it's okay.

"I haven't got anywhere I need to be," I say.

"Yay, we can watch Frozen and Tangled and can we watch Encanto too?" Seren asks.

"Of course," Joseph says.

I'm exhausted. The girls are lovely but they are really hard work. We managed to watch all three Disney films and even I now know the words to them. Joseph put the subtitles on and they sang along. So now we have tucked them in. Seren asked me to read to them and we slowly creep out of the room when they finally fall asleep.

"They are beautiful children," I say to Joseph, who brings in two wine glasses. This feels like déjà vu. I still can't get the image of his rejection out of my head even though it was so long ago now.

"They are, and although I wouldn't have been able to bring them up without my mum and dad," he

says.

He pours wine into both glasses and we toast. "To dreams coming true," I say. That sounds so cheesy. It must be all of those Disney films rubbing off on me.

"Definitely," he says and clashes our glasses. "So has yours come true?" he asks.

"Yes, I get to design dolls' clothes for the toy shop and I'm so excited," I say.

"My mum and dad have a really good eye for workers so you must have seriously impressed them," he says.

"I was so nervous I thought I was going to faint," I say and laugh. "The girls also came to test out my designs and tell me what they thought."

"I know. I did ask Mum if it was necessary but she said they are the target audience so who better to ask," he says.

"I can't believe I get to work on my designs. I can't help thinking about what Seren said," I start. Joseph looks at me with his lovely blue eyes.

"I'm sorry about that. She has been asking about her mum a lot lately," Joseph says.

"It's okay," I say with a nod.

"You see they lost their Mum near to Christmas so it's a very sensitive time of the year for us all," Joseph says.

"That makes sense," I say.

The air is quiet between us and I don't really know what to say. I've never been through this before.

"I was thinking about the dolls' house and I want to help with that. I want to help decorate it and give the girls some cute outfits for their dolls," I say.

"That sounds amazing, they are lucky that you came into their lives," he says.

"I was terrified to be in their lives before. I didn't think I could become anything in their lives," I say.

"Do you want to be something in their lives?" he asks. I feel him lean closer to me. Him being only a couple of inches from my face is distracting.

"I do," I whisper. "I want everything if it means I get to be with you."

He leans the rest of the way and we share a passionate kiss like that is what he wanted me to say. I'm really pleased I got that all out. It's nice to feel cleansed of my thoughts and know that he hasn't told me to get out of his house.

We pull away and he looks at me intensely with his deep blue eyes, like he has so much he wishes to say.

CHAPTER 20

"**S**o how do you like your eggs?" Joseph asks.

It's seven am and I'm in the hen house with Joseph. Gobble Di Gook has decided to join us and is fighting the hens for the feed.

The girls aren't awake yet and the sun is only just starting to come up. It's amazing how far it stretches on the farm.

"I like scrambled," I say with a smile.

"Go ahead see if there are any eggs," he says and opens the hatch. He follows me in and takes the chickens' food and water to fill up. The turkey is already waiting for more food. I do wonder if he is the pet or they will use him for Christmas?

The hens are already awake and walking around the house. I check all around while Joseph replaces the water and food. They all flock over to where Joseph is and he pets them.

"Say hello to Hen Solo, Princess Lay-an-egg, Kylo Hen, Darth Clucker, Chick Bacca, Obi Wan Henobi and Luke Ground Clucker," he says and picks one of them up stroking them.

I nervously walk over. Hens scare me with their little eyes. I stroke it and it feels soft and feathery. "Hello," I say. Joseph lets it go and I carry on walking around with the basket. I manage to find six eggs.

"Who's that?" Joseph asks, pointing to a silhouette coming towards the house. He takes my hand as we walk closer.

"Not sure," I say. It's still a little dark out so I wonder if it's someone from the village. Who would be calling this early?

"Hello?" Joseph calls and the figure turns around. I try not to gasp when I recognise my bloody ex-boyfriend.

"Hi, my name is Luke Blackburn I'm an environmental inspector, I'm going to be around for a couple of days inspecting," he says.

Joseph shakes hands with him but looks confused. Luke stares at me before readjusting his features and giving Joseph the biggest smile ever. A smile that used to make me weak but now just makes me want to hit him in his arrogant face.

"Sorry Holly, I will catch up with you later for lunch is that okay?" Joseph says and kisses my cheek. I can't look at Luke. I need a drink and it's only five in the morning.

❖ ❖ ❖

"Oh my god what is he doing here?" Jake asks. I'm in the pub with Melanie and Angel and Carol. I've filled them in on Luke.

"I don't know, I say. "Joseph just believed him, just like that."

"Well, he wouldn't have any reason to suspect him would he?" Melanie asks. The kids are playing in the pub garden while we sit next to the window watching them. It's freezing out and a layer of frost is sparkling on every surface. It's only midday and I'm dying to hear from Joseph.

"Should I tell Joseph who he is though?" I ask. The thought upsets me. I don't want to think that Joseph would be angry at me for knowing him but not saying anything.

"Yes," Melanie and Carol say.

"No," Jake says. "You should pull him aside and see what he's up to. I could beat it out of him if you want."

"No, I thought about doing that earlier but it's a waste of time and effort. How do I find out why he is here?" I ask.

"It's time for a little role play," Jake says. He looks at Melanie and Angel and they look at me. I feel goose bumps. I'm scared.

"What?" I ask.

"He's obviously come back to see you so why don't you pretend to be nice and find out what he is really here for and then tell Joseph," Jake says.

"I don't think it will work," I say.

"Of course it will," Jake says.

"It would be a good idea to warn him about what's going on," I say. "But I don't want Joseph to think something is going on with me and Luke. I don't want him to know that I know Luke at all. I don't want him to hurt Joseph or the girls just to get at me."

"What I want to know is how did he find you? This village isn't on the map and it's definitely not easy to find," Melanie asks.

I down the rest of my drink. I need the courage. How will I tell Joseph who Luke really is? Do I say that we are exes? Would it affect our relationship?

Joseph feels very new and very special to me and I want to tell everyone. Well, my mates at least who all asked for the details of my sleepover. They aahed and oohed when I told them but then I felt like I had betrayed Joseph's trust. Relationships are so confusing.

"We are going back to the hotel guys," Jake says, downing his own pint.

We all stand up getting ready to go.

"We'll come too," Angel says.

"You can't meet your ex wearing jeans and a baggy hoodie," Melanie says.

Jake looks way too excited as we all head into the hotel. We are grateful Carol decided to stay with the kids.

"I'm sorry, I can't tell you what Mr Blackburn is here for," Ivy says when I stop by the front desk to ask her.

My shoulders sag. "I guess that's it guys," I say.

"Not exactly. Come on let's go back to our room," Jake says and he leads us all upstairs.

"How do we even know he is staying here?" I ask.

"Where else will he stay?" Angel asks.

"So do we wait until we see him?" I ask.

"No, we dress you up first and then send you out there to get him," Jake says.

"I'm not wearing a short skirt in this weather," I protest. "Anyway I don't want to make him jealous or sleep with him, I just want to see what he is here for," I say.

"Yes, but that way he sees what he threw away," Jake says.

I sigh. I really don't care about him seeing me like that. I actually feel a bit sick about him being here. I'm still so angry at him for the way he treated me.

He didn't stop Kelly sacking me, even though he was the one cheating.

"I will wear a little make up but no skirts or dresses," I say, making it clear I'm not dressing up for Luke.

"Spoil sport, at least wear your heels," Jake says handing them to me. I roll my eyes and slip them on.

"He's going to know that I'm not just casually bumping into him," I say.

"I know that's why we are all getting dressed up, that way it looks like we are out celebrating," Angel says.

"We'll be there for an hour and then we've got to go back to the kids at the pub with Carol," Angel says.

"I have your back girl," Jake says slapping me on the back. I hate that they've encouraged me to do this.

I walk down to the hotel bar, feeling uncomfortable.

It isn't even definite he will be here anyway.

"Hello darling, are you here for lunch?" Ivy asks.

"Yes please, I need a table for four for lunch?" I say. She smiles though it doesn't reach her eyes and nods.

Have I upset her? I hope I haven't. I definitely don't want to do that.

Ivy comes back with menus for us all and everyone sits down.

"I fancy a cocktail," Jake says and orders the most extravagant looking one of the hotel. I raise my eyebrow at him.

"It's not even three in the afternoon," I say to Jake.

"Hey, who says you can't have a cocktail at three in the afternoon?" Jake says.

"I'll just have coffee," I say to Ivy. I've already had one pint and unlike Jake I don't plan on getting drunk.

"Can I just have water? I can't stay too long," Angel says.

"Me too," Melanie says.

I'm pleased I'm not the only one not drinking. I'm nervous as I look around and sure enough in he walks. He's changed out of his business suit and is now wearing a leather jacket and jeans. He looks like a complete bellend.

"There he is," I whisper to Angel. She doesn't look in the right direction and I have to point him out.

"He's hot," she whispers.

"He really isn't," I say.

It's weird how quickly you can go off of someone. If you take your rose-tinted glasses off and look at them you'll notice little things you didn't before. Or look back over the relationship and think of little things they did that would annoy you now but didn't then. It was never going to work.

"Quick, go and order something from the bar," Angel says. "And let me know what food you want."

"I will have another one of these please," Jake says holding his empty glass.

"I'll have pizza," I say and get up, pulling my jeans up and readjusting myself. I already know it's a bad idea wearing heels. Why did I let them talk me into this? I'm starting to feel the regret as I get closer to the bar.

I casually stand next to him getting ready to order and hoping he won't notice me. I know it's only been a few weeks since I last saw him but maybe he won't. I feel like a different person altogether.

"Hi, Holly," he says casually. He holds out his hand and the whole thing feels wrong.

"Hi," I say. I wish I had brought something with me. My hands curl up into nervous balls.

"So this is where you disappeared to?" he asks. I nod.

"Yeah, it's a really nice village full of lovely people." I emphasis lovely. It was lovely until he turned up anyway. "Why are you here Luke? And how did you find me?" I ask.

He rolls his eyes. "Always the accusations," he says. "I had a little help from my girlfriend, you know her right?" he says. I can sense the bitterness in his voice and pull a face. I'm not jealous. I am disgusted. I see him for who he really is.

"Of course I do," I say.

"She managed to convince your friends, the ones you would fob me off for, do you remember that? Anyway, Kelly paid them a little visit and told them if they didn't tell her where you had gone they were sacked," he says. He smirks like the cat that got the cream.

"But they quit so you had no hold over them," I finish his story and it's my turn to smirk.

"I found out overhearing their dumb conversations they were coming to see you so I followed them," he says.

I bite my lip. I didn't expect him to come here talking like this. Being nice to him really wasn't worth it.

"I thought you told me you didn't do your inspections over the festive period?" I ask. I don't know why I care. He was cheating on me anyway.

"Another lie, I wanted to be closer to Kelly and while you thought I was in the café I was actually finding out where you were so I could use my job to snoop around," he says.

"Very creative," I say sarcastically.

"Aren't you going to introduce me to your new friends?" he asks nodding towards my table.

"Nope," I say instantly.

He rolls his eyes. "For God's sake Holly you are so childish and pathetic, I don't know why I ever liked you," he says.

"Me, childish? I wasn't cheating on you and lying to you," I spit out. I can't believe he's calling me this.

"Yeah, yeah," he says rolling his eyes. "Anyway, it was actually Kelly's idea for me to come here and keep an eye on you. Funny that," he says with a hint of amusement.

"Well you can go back to Kelly, I don't want you here," I say. I am ready for Jake to come over and wipe the smug look off of Luke's face.

"Too bad," he whispers into my ear. I swallow the lump forming and smell the alcohol on his breath. "I already told you Holly, baby I'm here inspecting you're new mans farm." He wraps his arms around me so I can't move. I wonder if Angel and Melanie can see what he is trying to do. Luke forces his lips to mine.

I hear someone clearing their throat and Luke drops his hands from me.

"Oops, guess that's lover boy," he whispers. I see the look on Joseph's face. His eyes meet mine and he looks devastated. I won his trust and just like that it's shattered. His eyes are glassy and he looks close to tears.

I feel my heart drop into my stomach. He knew exactly what he was doing.

"I fucking hate you," I whisper before grabbing my bag and following Joseph out. Joseph walks fast and I have to keep up in these stupid heels.

"Joseph. Please wait," I cry and undo my shoes and carry them with me.

"I can't believe this, I can't believe you, do you know him?" He spins around to face me. I see the anger in his eyes and the hurt. I can't believe Luke knew he was there.

"Yes, he is the arsehole ex," I say.

"Doesn't seem to be an arsehole now, does he? You looked pretty snug together," he says. "I can't believe after everything I told you, after I let you into my home, into the girls' home and you were still going to kiss your ex," he says.

"No, I wasn't," I cry and Joseph walks away faster.

"Don't ever contact us again," he says.

I stand in the square and the tears come. I'm suddenly surrounded by Angel and Melanie.

They all put their arms around me as I cry. I can't believe Joseph thinks I would kiss another man.

"I shouldn't have fucking dressed up for such a dickhead," I say and run back to my hotel room. I throw my heels at the wall and stand in just my stupid top and jeans. How could I let them talk me into this? Why would I want to talk to Luke? I can't believe how mean he has been since he got here. I collapse on my bed, knowing I won't sleep a wink tonight.

CHAPTER 21

I must have eventually drifted off to sleep from exhaustion, when I wake up all the regrets come back. I can't believe Joseph would think I would go back to Luke. I drag myself up, knowing it's my first day at the workshop. Today will be positive. I will get stuck into my job and not think about the men. I get dressed in smart clothes and sort my face out. I put a smidge of lip gloss on and make sure my hair looks nice. I won't let any of this destroy my dream. I've been given the opportunity to do something that makes me happy and I am taking it.

I walk downstairs to the bar where my life went wrong and sit down.

"Morning Holly dear, I look forward to seeing you at the workshop," Ivy says with a smile. She puts her hand on my shoulder and I wonder if Joseph told her anything but then she hands me a bowl of porridge and walks away. She doesn't berate me for hurting her son at all so maybe not. I wouldn't blame her if she wanted to sack me. I'm so stupid.

I eat my food, having to force it down my throat,

before getting ready to walk up the hill.

The air is chilly and the wind hits like icicles stabbing my skin. The sky is a beautiful shade of pink and blue with the moon barely visible. I breathe out the cold air and the fog mists around me. My eyes water and it isn't just from the cold. How will I get through today knowing Joseph is only next door and I hurt him?

I walk up to the wooden door of the workshop. Do I knock? I do officially work here but I'm not sure how it works. I take my phone out of my bag with my lunch inside and check the time. I'm still really early. Should I go in and start or just wait? I look out towards the farm wondering if Joseph is out. Yesterday he was out on the farm earlier than this. I smile thinking of yesterday morning that was then ruined by Luke. We never did have our breakfast together. He hasn't texted me and I'm disappointed. I can't say I blame him though. I sigh and tap on the door. Ivy did say to start at six am but I'm not sure if anyone is in.

The door creaks slowly open and Ivy is standing there with Nick. They both smile at me.

"Welcome to the workshop, Holly," Nick says and holds his hand out and I shake it. His handshake is firm but friendly and I feel a little better but I'm still nervous.

"So I will take you for a tour around the workshop. The main room right here is split into sections as you can see by the signs. There is the woodwork and then the dolls that are personally knitted by our elves," Nick says.

"There's a uniform?" I ask seeing elf outfits hung on pegs by the door.

"Yes, we work in a workshop so I thought it would be a good idea to have a work uniform with name tags of course. You will get one Holly, Ivy already made one for you," Nick says.

"This is where you will be, over here in the designing section. So when the Fruity Tooties dolls we make are finished they will be passed to you. You will be working on that up to Christmas, after Christmas we will be making other dolls and teddies so we will have meetings about designs where we encourage employees to join in with ideas," Ivy says.

I walk over to my section that has a desk on it with a sewing machine. I look around and see a cupboard and open it. It's full of loads of different material, every colour and texture imaginable. I'm going to love it here. I also see books with toy ideas inside them in case I get stuck. There's pencils and paper in a pigeon hole behind the sewing machine.

"If you need anything you can call us anytime. We have phones next to each of the workshop sections. You just press 2512 and it will ring us," she says. I see the phone she means neatly placed on the side.

"Do you want to go and grab a drink and get started on the first dolls' clothes?" Ivy asks.

"Yes please," I say.

"Oh, one more thing," she says turning around to face me. I freeze midway through taking my coat off.

"At ten we all have a hot chocolate break," she says.

Its midday and I'm sitting at my sewing machine eating an apple. It's been a bit of a hectic day. I've loved every minute of it but I can't help but miss Joseph. I'm only two seconds away from the farm and it's so annoying that I'm so close but so far.

Everyone else has gone out for dinner including Ivy and Nick so it's just me here. I told them I wasn't going anywhere so they didn't lock up. Only people who work here have seen inside so it's really secret.

I look at my design of 'Strawberry' the red doll that has cute little freckles on her face. Her hair is green and spiky just like the top of a strawberry. Her dress is red with yellow spots on top with sleeves that ruffle and a skirt that puffs out like a ballet tutu. I've got the top part done and now I've finished my apple and washed my hands it's time to fit the top onto the doll. I pull it over its head and it fits perfectly. I smile at my own design. I can't believe I'm designing clothes for this new range. It still doesn't feel real. I cut my lunch break short to ruffle up the red tutu material and stitch it together . I don't even notice everyone else coming back in after their breaks.

"How are you getting on, love?" Ivy asks.

"I'm good, I've done the strawberry design now," I say and show her.

"That's amazing," she says. "Nick, come and look at this," she says.

Minutes later Nick comes in and sees what I've been working on.

"These designs are fantastic, Ivy has a good eye for workers," he says.

"I do," she says and they kiss. I feel like I'm interrupting a moment and go back to work.

"So, how many of these am I making?" I ask. I've seen that I've got to make lots of dolls but not how many altogether.

"Fifty," she says.

"Will I have time before Christmas?" I ask.

"Oh she of little faith, of course you will," Nick says.

"I agree with Nick. You are amazing at what you do," Ivy says.

I feel a little more positive but I'm still nervous. What if we don't make them in time?

"When do the dolls go on sale?" I ask.

"In three days," Ivy says, looking to Nick who nods.

"Three days to make fifty dolls?" I ask. I feel sick with nerves again. Oh god, what have I agreed to?

"Don't look so scared, you have a team with you to help you. Marley over there is making some of the banana designs that you've given to us, and Bella over there is making an orange outfit using the images that you showed us. I hope you don't mind that they are using your designs," Ivy says.

I look around at Marley and Bella who have some of the fabric for the top of the banana. It's exactly like my design.

"No, of course I don't mind," I say. I can't believe other people are making my dolls' clothes with my drawings. My little scribbles are finally getting me somewhere.

"When they are made we are having an opening day at the toy shop. I've already made some posters and when one of each of them is done our photographer Nelle will take a professional photo for our marketing," Ivy says.

I nod, trying to process it all. I feel like I'm stuck in a dream

I walk out of the workshop feeling amazing. It's a high I would never have been able to achieve from

anything apart from following my own dreams.

The sun is going down over the hills and I can't help but notice how beautiful it looks. I could sit here and watch it completely darken and never get sick of the view. I can't believe I get to work here every day and see this view. A warm feeling washes over me as I tighten my coat around me. The air is biting and I want to get back to the hotel and maybe eat chocolate ice cream to celebrate.

"Holly?"

I turn around and see Luke coming my way. He doesn't look as smug as yesterday. Maybe he's managed to stay sober today.

"What do you want, Luke?" I say crossing my arms.

"Can we walk and talk please?" he asks. He puts his hand to my back and I move away. I can't stand the slime ball touching me.

"We can walk, yes," I say and he keeps up pace beside me.

"I just want to say I'm kind of sorry for last night. We got off on the wrong foot," he says.

"You broke up my new relationship. How did we get off on the wrong foot?" I ask. I want to kick him and run back to my room but that isn't the mature way to deal with it. Do I really want to hear what he has to say?

"I know," he says. I see him running his hands through his hair. Something I used to love doing.

His hair was so thick and it was beautiful… I shake my head to rid myself of the bad thoughts. I don't like this man.

"What did you come to say?" I ask.

"We really are cutting straight to the point. I've come to do my job. I have to assess complaints and low and behold there was a complaint," he says with a shrug.

"Who complained?" I demand.

"Kelly," he says.

"Of course, why am I so surprised?" I ask. I feel disgusted with him.

"Oh come on, Holls, you didn't think I could actually stay with you, you're basically a child. When something didn't work you would strop. And you are fucking obsessed with Christmas for fuck's sake," Luke says.

"Why do you hate that I love Christmas so much?" I ask.

"Because it isn't fucking normal for adults to love Christmas so much," he says.

I feel the tears prickle my eyes. Why was he ruining my day? Why couldn't he just go home?

"Not everyone is a scrooge," I say defensively.

"Don't get me wrong, I like Christmas but I hate that Christmas shop you work at. Kelly and I were going to tell you about us but then you walked in on us and Kelly sacked you. When we found out how happy you were here we decided to sack off your stupid friends," he says.

"You are worse than evil," I say.

We reach the hotel and I want to go inside and disappear.

"Maybe, but I want to make you feel something different. Make you grow up a little. So I am really going to hurt you just like you hurt me every time you decorated my flat for Christmas or bought me a tacky Christmas present. I am going to fail your boyfriend and then bye bye farm," he says.

"You can't do that to him," I say.

He grabs me and pulls me closer to him. I want to bite his nose off but he is holding me too tightly. A couple of visitors walk by and think we are gazing into each other's eyes. I hear "Awe, how sweet!" and I feel physically sick.

"I will do it and if you tell him I will get your pathetic workshop closed down too," he says. I push him away and Jake punches him. Luke falls backwards on the floor with Jake standing over him.

"How much did you hear?" I ask.

"I heard all of it," he says. He starts playing it on his phone. "You need to tell Joseph."

Carol comes over and hugs me.

"I'm so sorry he followed us," she says.

Jake joins in with the hug. "It's okay. I'm sorry that you had no choice but to quit your jobs," I say.

"Well, about that," they say and I look at both of them.

CHAPTER 22

"OMG, guys that is amazing," I say. We sit outside the hotel talking and I hug each of them. It's freezing now and I'm still a little shaken up by Luke but it's slowly fading thanks to their news.

"I start as a teacher after Christmas," Jake says.

"I start at the bakery tomorrow," Carol says.

"I can't believe you are going to be staying here with me," I say.

"Neither can we, and look at you the famous fashion designer. Will you still remember us when you're famous?" Jake says.

I laugh. "Of course," I say.

"We should really tell Joseph what is going on," Carol says.

"But what if Luke does what he says? What if he shuts the workshop down?" I ask.

"He isn't going to shut the farm or workshop down," Jake says.

I see him and Carol exchange looks.

"Go now and talk to Joseph, I'll stay here in case pretty boy wakes up again," Jake says.

"I need to go to bed early for tomorrow, did you know I will be starting at three am?" Carol says. I smile at them as I head for the farm. Once I've retraced my steps I nervously knock on the door.

I hear shuffling and the door opens. Joseph is standing in his pajamas. His hair is messy and he looks crap.

"What do you want?" he asks with sharpness in his voice.

"I need to talk to you," I say desperately. "It involves your parents too."

"So the man is only here to get revenge on you?" Ivy says, looking anxious. Joseph holds her hand and her face is pale with worry.

"I've a good mind to go and see him myself," Nick says.

"No, Dad, that won't help anything will it? Remember, it's the season of goodwill," Joseph says. Nick sits back down grumpily.

"He threatened to shut down the workshop if I said anything but I couldn't just let him ruin your livelihood," I say to Joseph. He looks up at me and I see the worry and concern in his eyes.

"You shouldn't put yourself at risk," he says. He rushes over to me and hugs me. I hug him. Even if he can't like me again at least I saved his home. It makes me feel better about everything.

"I had to. You can't lose everything, not with the girls. Even if you hate me now at least I know I did the right thing," I say.

"I will get onto the council tomorrow and sort it out, I think for safety you need to stay here tonight," Ivy says.

I nod. "I'm exhausted," I yawn.

"Have you eaten tonight?" Joseph asks. I shake my head.

"Well, luckily we made too much pasta tonight," Ivy says and goes off to make me a bowl. I smile at their generosity. Even when they are worrying they still think of other people.

I can see the farm from the window and it all looks so peaceful.

I shake myself awake. It's dark outside. That's weird. I can smell something, too. Are they cooking breakfast? I get up and pad on over to the kitchen that overlooks the workshop. I see smoke coming out of the farm barn.

Oh shit. All of the animals will be inside there.

"Joseph!" I yell, running up to his bedroom. I see from outside of his window the smoke is getting nearer. The animals are all in a frenzy trying to escape. I don't think I've ever heard a pig scream but that must be the terrible sound I can hear.

I shake Joseph awake and show him outside. He quickly gets up to go and sort the animals.

"Wake Mum and Dad, please," he says and disappears out of the door.

"Ivy, Nick, someone has set fire to the farm," I shout. I turn the lights on and they stir.

They climb out of bed as quickly as they can and go to help Joseph.

"Stay with the girls in case they wake up," Ivy says leaving me in the dark house. I shiver with fear as I go around turning lights on. I can't sit in the house on my own in the dark.

I hear the letterbox clatter and a voice coming through it.

"Oh Holly, Holly, Holly, you thought you would be clever. Well, not anymore. See I told you what would happen if you told Joseph, so really this is your fault." I can't see him through the hallway window but I see through the glass door something bright. What is he doing?

The letterbox moves and I see Luke has thrown something on fire through the letterbox. My first thought is the girls.

I can't see Joseph, Ivy or Nick at all but I can get the girls out. The fire starts spreading down the hallway. I quickly climb up the stairs and into the girls' bedrooms.

"Seren, Star, we need to get out of the house," I say.

I carry both of the girls down the stairs. How do I get out? The fire has now reached the living room but the kitchen is still free. The girls start moving in my arms. I run through the kitchen and fling open the backdoor running out of it and around the side of the house.

I ring the fire brigade and text everyone in the village to come and help me. I place the girls softly down on the bench to sleep.

Minutes later Carol and Jake run over to me. Jake takes off his jacket and covers the girls with it.

I cry into Jake's arms and the girls stir awake now. The cold must have made them wake up and they start crying too. Carol sits with them and tells them a story.

"We want Daddy," Seren cries.

"Daddy," Star wails. I look to Carol and bite my lip. Where are they?

The police and fire fighters come and two figures run back to us. Joseph is holding Gobble Di Gook covered in ash. He smells like smoke and part of his feathers are black.

"What happened?" Joseph asks. He runs to the girls

and pulls them into his arms. I take the turkey and put him on the floor. Joseph is covered in ash and stinks of smoke. I can see his dressing gown has burnt holes in it and I wonder how he managed to get out.

"Luke set fire to the house," I say with tears running down my eyes. "I'm so sorry for everything."

"Shh. It's okay, it isn't your fault," Joseph says.

"Where is Nick?" I ask.

Joseph points to the ambulance driving down the lane.

"My dad's just had a heart attack," he says. I see the tears in his eyes. I can't believe all of this has happened on one night. It's so surreal. Nick is the heart of the village. Without him I wouldn't want to think about what it would be like.

"I'm so sorry," I say and hug him. He kisses my cheek.

"I'm also sorry," he says and we watch the firefighters putting the fire out. Ivy has gone with Nick so Joseph, with the help of Jake carries the girls to the hotel. Luckily the police have caught Luke and he is now in the back of their car. I can't believe I ever liked someone who could treat other people like this. He could have really hurt someone. Joseph tells me that because of my eager eye none of the animals got hurt and because my fast reactions the girls are completely fine.

"You can't stay on your own tonight," Joseph says. He locks his fingers into mine and squeezes. I am visibly shaking and I'm not sure if it's the cold or the shock of tonight but I squeeze his hand back feeling a little reassured.

"This is all my fault," I say. "Everything is because Luke wanted to hurt me."

Joseph holds me tight and I cry against him. Someone could have been killed. The girls could have been really hurt.

"Because of you though, everything is okay," Joseph says smoothing my hair down.

"Because of me your dad's in hospital," I say against him.

"I know," he says. I don't know how but I eventually manage to fall asleep.

A knock on the door stirs me.

"Holly, are you awake?" I hear Carol from outside the door.

"I told you, it's too early," Jake whispers.

"Guys just go in there," Joseph says. I pull the quilt higher up to over me and sit up. My friends come into the room holding plates.

"We thought you would want to have a nice

breakfast with us," Carol says.

"I helped too," Seren says carrying a cup.

"Me too," Star says.

I smile as they all sit on the bed, plating up food.

"I can't believe you all did this," I say and hug them.

"We wanted to make sure you were okay after last night," Joseph says.

He puts his arms around me and I rest my head against him.

"How is your dad doing?" I ask. I feel awful about how everything happened and although they tell me not to blame myself, if Luke hadn't followed me none of this would have happened.

"He's telling the hospital that they are making a lot of hassle for nothing so I think he's okay. They want to check him over and make sure they haven't missed anything," he says.

I smile. "I'm really pleased he's okay."
"He has asked you to take the morning off of work to go and see him so we are going to take the girls if that's okay?" he asks.

"You're asking me if you can take your girls to see their granddad?" I ask.

"Yes, and then when you finish work this afternoon I want you to come back here with us," he says. He kisses the top of my head and I hear Carol and Jake aah.

"Guy, shut up," I say and roll my eyes.

"Well, I can't hang around you love birds anyway," Jake says.

"Why, what are you two doing today?" I ask. Joseph gets up to get the girls ready while I finish eating my breakfast.

"I've got some training to do to be a teacher," Jake says.

"And I need to get to the bakery," Carol says.

"So you are actually moving to the village then? Where will you stay?" I ask. I have so many questions.

"Don't worry about that," Jake says.

"I'm so sorry guys, for all of it," I say and they pull me into a hug.

"You have nothing to be sorry for," Carol says.

"Just try to pick better men," Jake adds.

We laugh and I realise how much I need my friends with me. It's so nice that they want to stay here with me.

"Meet us at the pub later. We might have news," Carol says and squeezes me once more.

The following morning I get out of bed and look out of the window. The sky is white and flurries of snow are fluttering down on the dry ground. It's snowing and it's only four days until Christmas. I've never really cared about having a white Christmas. They are always what you would expect in a film at the end with everyone living happily ever after. But now I really want it to snow on Christmas. It somehow feels like it would be more magical if it snows and I know the girls would love it too.

CHAPTER 23

It's weird sitting in the car holding Joseph's hand while Wizzard is playing through the speakers. The girls are singing along and I smile as I catch Joseph's eye. I feel like I'm part of their family and that feeling is so precious to me. It's better than when I first came here and I tried to fit in. I've found my place now and I don't want to be anywhere else.

"So, was there a reason your dad wants to see me?" I ask. We finally pull up at the hospital and the nerves kick in.

"I'm not sure," he says.

I have a horrible feeling in my gut but I don't want to ruin anything. What if I lose my dream job? This was all my fault and Nick wouldn't be in hospital if it wasn't for me.

"I hope it isn't anything bad," I say, voicing my concern. Joseph kisses me on the cheek and the girls want to hold my hands.

"It definitely won't be anything bad," he says and we head inside.

I haven't been into a hospital in so long. They actually scare me a little. I think with the high ceilings and the lack of natural light it feels claustrophobic.

"I'm going to head in first, is that okay?" Joseph asks when we reach the sitting area. I nod and let the girls pick a flavoured drink from the machine. Joseph disappears and I keep my fingers crossed that everything is okay. I really like Joseph and his family and I want to stay in their lives. I want to see the girls getting older and be there when they need someone. However complicated it might be.

The guilt of it all is eating me alive and I really want to do something to help with the cost of repairs. Luckily nothing major got destroyed in the farm and all of the animals are fine but the house is burnt and needs some repairing. I can't help feel it's my fault and I really want to make up for it.

"You can come in," Joseph whispers. He smiles and squeezes my hand. I feel the nerves twist in my gut. What if they blame me and send me away?

"Oh Holly, darling," Ivy rushes over and hugs me. "Are you okay my love?"

I can't believe she is asking about me when her husband is in hospital.

"Is Nick okay? I'm so sorry about everything," I say. I feel the tears coming already.

"Yes love, I've told him about his diet so many

times," she says, shaking her head.

"There is nothing wrong with my diet," Nick grumbles.

"Grandpa!" The girls run over to him and he hugs them.

"Gentle girls grandpa isn't well," Ivy says and joins the hug. Joseph comes over and joins in too.

"Nick, I am so sorry for everything," I start. Nick puts his hand up to stop me.

"Holly, I didn't want you to come and see me to say sorry. In fact if it wasn't for you, I'm not sure what would have happened. You saved my family, my son and our granddaughters," he says.

I see Ivy nod and my eyes tear up again. They are thanking me. I can't actually believe this.

"You really don't have to thank me, I'm so truly grateful for everything you have done for me," I say.

"When I finally get out of this damned place I want to set up a meeting with you. This has been a long time coming," Nick says to me but looks to Ivy whose hand he is holding.

"You've finally decided to listen then?" Ivy says.

"Yes," he says.

Joseph gets up and hugs his dad again. "Get better Dad. Don't worry about anything else."

"I will," Nick says and nods.

I walk over and he squeezes my hand. "I will be out in time for our launch of the dolls."

I look over to Ivy. "When is the launch of the dolls?" I ask.

"Saturday," she says.

I bite my lip. We've only made a couple of them and we only have a day to get them out there.

"We will do it in time don't you worry," Ivy says.

CHAPTER 24

We are sitting in the meeting the day before our launch. I can't stop thinking about the fire and how everything is my fault. Even Gobble Di Gook being injured is my fault and I feel bad for him. Luckily he's okay.

"So with our launch at the toy shop tomorrow, does anyone have any launch ideas?" Mack who works with us on the designs asks us.

Joseph has dropped me off at the workshop and I am just in time for the hot chocolate meeting. Ivy has a link to the meeting and is watching it online with Nick even though they probably shouldn't be. I love their dedication to their jobs.

No one says anything. I look around at the table at us all in our elf costumes that are bright red and green. No one has anything to say at all. I don't even have to sense anything to know Ivy would be disappointed.

"We should do a party with ribbon at the door and then the dolls should be the main focus of the event. We could get some food and cakes made by the local villagers for the event," I say and look around. Everyone is chattering.

"That is fantastic. Ivy, what do you think?" Mack asks.

Ivy appears on the big screen with Nick next to her. They have carefully avoided the hospital equipment in the background.

"I think that sounds great, Holly, we will discuss this more when I get home. I want to know how far we are with the dolls," she says.

We bring over a box of dolls and pick a couple up. They are floppy and the outfits are really bright and colourful.

"They look amazing," Ivy says, her face lighting up. I feel a sense of accomplishment.

"We've been working overtime and through our breaks to finish these," Mack says.

"We are about half way through the banana ones," I update Ivy.

"Great, thank you everyone for the update. And thank you all for your hard work," Ivy says.

We disconnect the video.

"You heard Ivy, back to work everyone," Mack says.

We all shuffle back into our areas.

I can't help but think of Joseph and how he almost lost everything in the fire but he's still so upbeat. I really want to do something nice for them. I finish sewing the last of my banana dress as I think about it.

I could try to raise money in the village. I could busk on the square when my shift is over in my Christmas outfit. Everyone would help the family who pretty much run the village.

As my fingers ache and I turn the sewing machine off for the day, I think about it some more. It's getting dark outside already and I dress the banana doll and put her in the box with the others. I don't want Ivy to come home and see me busk for money. She would never accept it.

Everyone else has already left except for Mack who is waiting outside the workshop for me to come out. I gather my stuff, still in my work uniform and put my coat on. The snow has coated the ground outside in a light dusting that looks like icing sugar. It crunches under my foot as I step out.

"See you tomorrow," he says and heads towards the car park. I follow the path down the hill and onto the square. Shop lights are still on and I see a couple of the shop owners still serving customers. I nervously stand in the square on the little grassy area and put down my pot. I quickly make a sign saying 'Funds for Ivy and Nick' and hold it while I start singing 'Santa Claus Is Coming To Town'

Within a few minutes I'm surrounded by villagers. It feels a little like Elf. Families are swaying and a couple are joining in.

Angel and Carol come out of the bakery and join in

and everyone eventually starts singing along.

"What shall we sing next?" I ask the crowds.

"All I Want For Christmas Is You?" Carol shouts.

"Yeah!" Mr Tree comes over with Jake and holds his thumbs up mouthing he got the job. I'm so proud of him to be working with the children that I worked with. He's finally using his degree that he worked so hard for.

We put our arms around each other and I really feel the Christmas spirit as we sway and sing. More people from the village join us and the snow starts falling again. The Christmas lights hung around the shops and around the lamp posts shine brightly and I'm blown away by how hallmark the setting is.

CHAPTER 25

Nick and Ivy come to the hotel the next morning as I'm eating a yummy bacon sandwich with Seren and Star.

"Good morning everyone," Ivy says.

Nick wheels in on his wheelchair.

"Dad, are you okay?" Joseph gets up and helps him.

"Can I have some breakfast?" he asks.

"Now, Nick dear, you need to cut down the fat remember?" Ivy says.

"Would you like some cereal Dad?" Joseph asks.

"You can have some of my cornflakes grandpa," Seren says.

"Or my Cocopops," Star adds.

"Yes please girls," Nick says.

"I'll do it Dad," Joseph says. Ivy pushes him closer to the table and Joseph makes him a bowl of cereal.

"I don't need everyone to look after me," Nick grumbles.

"Nick dear, your family want to be here for you and you need all of the energy for our meeting today. We are going to discuss the details on the launch of our dolls," she says.

"I can't wait for them to be in the shops," I say with a smile. All of my hard work has been for this.

"Can we see them?" Star asks.

"You can see them later when we release them, girls," Ivy says. "You will be there, won't you son?"

"Of course Mum I wouldn't miss your new line for anything. Or yours," he adds and kisses me in front of his parents. I can't help blushing. I'm not used to an audience and definitely not Joseph's mum and dad.

"That's my boy," Nick says.

"So I was going to wait a little while to tell you this," I start.

They look at me expectantly.

"But I want to give you this. Thank you for everything you have done for me. You've helped me find my way and discover my dreams. I have managed to raise some money for the repairs to the house and I know you both say it isn't my fault but I wanted to help in any way I could," I say.

I hand them a pot full of money.

"I'm sorry if it doesn't do much but I want to help repair your home. You've lived there all your lives and I want the girls to have their home back," I say.

I see tears in Ivy and Nick's eyes and even Joseph wipes his eyes.

"My darling, this is enough to fix our home," Ivy says. She hugs Nick sobbing and they pull me into a hug.

"I just want the girls to have their home back. I know they enjoy staying here but it can't be good for them," I say.

"There's nothing more I want than us being safely back in our home again," Ivy says.

"Me too, Mum." Joseph says.

We all hug again and Joseph kisses me again in front of his mum and dad. This time I don't mind though. I want to spend my life with this man and his family. I love them all so much. I can't believe we've all been through so much together.

It's launch day and also two days before Christmas and all I am thinking about is my new role in this village, my new role with the girls and how I no longer feel like they are going to get in my way or that Joseph has to choose me or them because I feel like we are in this together. Joseph has let me into his life and his heart. The man who drank himself to sleep every night has finally let me in. The thought makes me fuzzy and warm. I love that he has let me into his life.

It's below freezing, the snow is still coming down heavily, and the girls are still fast asleep. I get my winter gear and hats and gloves on with Joseph as we bring woolly coats and electric heaters for some of the animals. Gobble Di Gook is being kept inside as it's too cold for him now and he has a spare room in the conservatory with a brooder and his food.

"I think we've earnt a cup of tea and a biscuit don't you?" Joseph asks. We put the last coat on Sausage and Bacon and head back into the house. It still smells ever so slightly burnt but Joseph has worked hard repairing the lounge and repainting the walls thanks to the money the villagers and I raised for them. Joseph flicks the kettle on and I go and check on the girls. They are still fast asleep under their canopy beds. I smile as I creep back down to the kitchen.

"So, how are you feeling about today?" he asks. He puts a steamy cup in front of me and then stacks two bourbons on top of each other.

"I'm so nervous," I say and bite my lip. Joseph sits next to me and bites into his own biscuit.

"There's no need to be nervous. Everyone is going to love the dolls," he says.

"But what if no one turns up?" I ask. I feel way too nervous even to eat bourbons and that's saying something.

"Mum told everyone about it. Believe me, everyone

will be there," Joseph says.

"What if they don't like them then?" I ask.

Joseph threads his fingers through mine and kisses me. "You worry too much," he says.

I nibble the end of my bourbon feeling sick. We've only got a few hours until the launch and I still need to make sure the catering is coming. Angel and Carol are making little fruit cakes for the launch. I wonder how many will come today and my stomach tightens again. I'm so scared. This is my dream and it's something I've wanted all my life and now I have it I'm terrified.

I down the rest of my tea.

"I need to go and get changed," I say to Joseph who has finished eating and is now halfway out of the door.

"Please have a shower before you come to the shop," I say and kiss him. Joseph smiles after kissing me.

"Of course I will," he says. "The girls can't wait to see the dolls."

I leave Joseph and go for a shower. The water is hot and I soak for a few minutes thinking about today. Surely Ivy and Nick wouldn't want me to do this if they didn't believe I would do well? They seem to have so much faith in me. Maybe I should have more faith in myself.

I get out and dry myself, changing into a black

dress and red cardigan. I want to make an effort. I style my hair and even slap a little make up on.

"Holly, you look pretty," Seren says and lifts her arms. I pick her up and hug her, squeezing her little body and I smile. They are beautiful little girls.

"Can I do your hair Holly?" she asks running her hands through it. I smile at her. I've already done it but what harm can it be?

"Of course," I say and she wriggles down and grabs her Barbie hair brush.

"You'll regret it," Joseph whispers while I get bossed around by two four- year- olds. I feel them tugging my hair and my head actually hurts by the time they are done with me.

"You look..." Joseph says and I can tell by his face he doesn't know whether to laugh or be serious.

"I'm a little scared," I whisper.

"Okay girls, go and get your faces wiped and come back down please," Joseph says. He gives me a mirror and the girls have twisted my hair in all different places. Joseph helps undo the ties and I brush them out.

"You look amazing. Stop worrying so much," he says.

"I just want today to be good, no I want it to be perfect and I want you all there to see it," I say.

"I wouldn't miss it for the world," he says and cups

my face. He leans in and kisses me and I still can't get over the fact I have this lovely man.

"Eww," Star says and Joseph pulls away slowly and smiles.

"Okay girls," Joseph says.

"Daddy and Holly kissing, yuck yuck yucky," Star says and they both giggle.

I laugh and hug them both. "Do you love my daddy?" Seren asks and I see Joseph going red.

"Holly loves Daddy, Holly Loves Daddy." They start running rings around us. I feel exhausted already but I know if I'm with Joseph then I can learn how to be involved in the girls lives. I would never want to replace their mum but I hope to be a positive influence in their lives. I love being around them so much.

"Welcome everyone." Ivy has a microphone at a podium. I have no idea how she got it there or set it up but she looks like a politician in her skirt suit. Nick is sitting next to her in a wheelchair and there is red ribbon around the toy shop. It seems like everyone got the memo and are gathered outside the toy shop. The snow has fallen through the night and a decent layer of it is on the ground. Seren and Star are trying to make snow angels as Joseph is trying to get them to listen to their grandma.

"Can Holly Willows please come up to the podium?" Ivy says and I make my way to the front. All eyes are on me and I hear Melanie and Angel cheering.

"Hi everyone I want to welcome you to the launch of the Fruity Tooties. The dolls that are based around your favourite fruit. I'm the designer of the outfits and I really hope you like the dolls today," I say.

Ivy squeezes my arm proudly.

"I'm proud of you kid," Nick whispers.

"If you would all like to come this way, Holly will cut the rope," Ivy says.

Ivy gives me her scissors and we all count down from ten. Seren and Star are at the front with Joseph and he kisses my cheek after I've snipped it.

I hold his hand and Seren's as Joseph holds Star's hand. To anyone else we look like a real family. My heart feels full when I think about feeling like a family. I've never really felt like I fit in anywhere but I seem to fit straight in here and even Jake and Carol have decided to stay.

"I'm so sorry I'm a little late." Carol comes through the door holding trays.

Angel and Melanie have trays each too.

"Where shall we put them Holls?" Carol asks.

"On the table," I say.

I set up a huge table by the window last night with Ivy's help and everyone can have a fruity cake that matches the dolls and champagne of the best kind.

"Everyone grab yourself a drink and browse for yourselves," I say and the crowd cheers.

Jake comes over to me, holding a glass of champagne.

"I'm so proud of you," he says and hugs me, spilling champagne on me.

"How many of those have you had?" I ask.

"Only two Sherlock," he says.

"Jake, can you slow down on the champagne a little?" I whisper.

"I know," he says and I leave him next to the cakes. I know he got the teaching job and he wants to celebrate but today isn't the right time to get drunk.

"I'm so damn proud of you girl," Angel says after putting the cakes down with the champagne.

"Mum, I'm bored," Jude says.

"Go and look around for Christmas presents," Angel says.

"You'll regret that," I say.

"Yeah, I know, but it stops him nagging me," she says. "It's a shame I never had a girl, isn't it?"

"I know, I can't believe the dolls are selling," I say. I look over to the shelf at the marketing we made the last two days, and the shelves are already emptying. They are selling faster than the cakes can be eaten.

"I'm going to stick some music on," Ivy says and whizzes away.

"Can I have everyone's attention?" Nick says.

He has been complaining about being in a wheelchair but we are so pleased he's alive and mostly well after the heart attack had has left him paralyzed down one side. The doctors didn't know until they tried to get him to walk and he just couldn't. But we have him here and I couldn't think of a better person to be my boss. Nick has been absolutely amazing with my contribution to the dolls and helping everything go smoothly even if Ivy tells him to rest.

"I want to make an announcement, I'm retiring as CEO of Claus Productions. I want to appoint our new manager of the workshop," Nick says and I hear a drum roll through the intercom.

"Holly," Ivy and Nick say.

"What?" I turn around to face them. I am head manager of the workshop.

"I can't be a manager! I've not even been here a month," I stutter.

"Congratulations," Joseph says and picks me up,

spinning me around and kissing me.

"Welcome to the family, Holly," Nick says. I feel the tears in my eyes as I hug him. I'm a part of this family and I can't think of anything I'd rather have.

CHAPTER 26

It's Christmas Eve and I'm more excited than the girls.

"Can we watch Frozen before we go to bed?" Seren asks.

"I want to leave the cookies and milk for Santa first," Star says.

It feels so strange. The house is all sorted out and repainted and everything is almost back to normal. Well except Nick who's still in his chair. I can't believe I'm going to be head of the workshop starting after Christmas. I realise how much I'll have to do but I'm ready for the challenge.

"Girls, we can do both, right Joseph?" I ask.

"Of course," he says.

I let the girls pour the milk and get the cookies out and we place the plate on the living room table.

"Can you stay with us until we fall asleep?" Star asks.

I help Joseph get the girls into their pajamas and we settle in beside them. Joseph holds my hand as the girls get progressively more tired. I've never been so happy in my life and I can't wait to show the girls what I got them for Christmas.

"Holly, psst are you awake?" A voice disturbs me and I realise I had fallen asleep next to Star.

"Yeah," I whisper and I feel a hand grab for me.

"Let's go to bed," Joseph says and leads me to the bedroom.

I follow him, my hand in his and the feeling rises up inside me of being warm and at ease. I've never really known where I belong and right now I've finally found the person I want to be with.

We get into bed together and I wrap my arms around him.

"Holly?" he whispers even though we are in the same room and the girls are down the hall.

"Yes," I say.

"I love you," he whispers and we kiss this time desperately and lovingly.

"I love you too," I say.

I've never really spent Christmas with children before. Of course, I've seen it on the TV and heard from Melanie that usually they are up at three am opening presents and someone's stressing over cooking the turkey. My Christmas mornings usually consist of being hungover and waking up with Carol and Jake at one of our houses ready to party again. By four am, Melanie is texting to ask whether the girls are up. It's silent in the house so I get up and potter down to the kitchen to have a cup of tea. I'm even more excited than the girls to see the presents they get today.

I flick the switch of the kettle on and sit down waiting for it to boil. Still nothing upstairs. What time does everyone usually wake up? I text Melanie to tell her no one is awake and she calls me lucky. I am lucky. I smile, looking out of the kitchen window at the dark sky that overlooks the farm. I'm very lucky. I can't believe I have all of this. What did I do to deserve this?

I hear creaking at the stairs and wait to see who it is.

Joseph opens the kitchen door wearing a red plaid shirt and jeans

"Merry Christmas," he says and pulls me into his arms, kissing me.

"Merry Christmas, do you want a cuppa?" I ask adding another cup next to mine and filling it with a tea bag and sugar, without waiting for an answer.

"Please," he says. He folds his arms through mine and I smile.

"Do you want to help me with the animals?" Joseph asks.

When I can't sleep and I wake up early enough it's one of my favourite things to help out on the farm. Everything is so quiet and peaceful and I love watching the sun come up behind the hills.

This morning though it seems to have snowed a little bit more as fresh powdery snow has settled and the picturesque farm is now full of it.

It's absolutely freezing so I grab my winter coat and gloves and follow Joseph, who is only wearing his shirt and jeans.

"Aren't you cold?" I ask. I'm shivering and I can already feel the coldness biting at my cheek.

"No," he says and I follow him to the animals.

I just want to grab his hand and hug him forever.

"Merry Christmas, girls," I say when we come back into the house an hour later and they are heading down the stairs. Joseph flicks the heating on to warm the house and we go around turning the lights on so it looks like someone actually lives here.

"Has Santa come, Holly?" Star asks. She holds her arms out and I pick her up. She plants a sloppy kiss on my cheek and I laugh. I get to spend Christmas with these beautiful little girls and I can't think of anything better.

"Let's go and see shall we?" I say and follow Joseph

into the living room.

"Morning Ivy, Nick," I say and Ivy kisses my cheek and then takes Star out of my arms.

"My my girls, it seems that you've been very good this year," Nick says and he winks at me. I smile.

"You too, love," he says to me.

Nick hands me a stack of presents.

"I didn't expect anything," I say. I feel the tears in my eyes. I can't believe they got me presents.

"Of course we got you presents," Ivy says.

"WE didn't get you anything. It's all from Santa," Nick says.

"Can we open this first?" Seren and Star are pulling along a really big present and I look to Joseph. Joseph has no idea what I did in my spare time for the girls but I really hope they like it.

"You must have been really good this year," Nick says.

The girls tear off the paper and their dolls' house they showed me a week ago is under there. "Did Santa get confused?" Star asks.

"No Star, look," Seren says and they both look inside. I helped wallpaper the house and make it look pretty. The toy girls are wearing new outfits that I made for them and toy Joseph is wearing a suit.

"Our dolls are dressed Daddy, even you," Seren

says.

Joseph takes the dolls and looks at me. "Did you do that?" Joseph asks.

"Yes, Merry Christmas girls," I say.

"Can we give Holly our present?" Star asks.

"Yes, the girls wanted to get you something and so did I. Before you protest, we want you to feel a part of our lives," Joseph says and takes my hand.

"Here you go Holly," Seren says.

They watch me like a hawk and I open the paper. The doll looks like me.

"It's me!" I laugh and tears come out of my eyes.

"You can join our house with Daddy and Grandma Ivy made you a dress," Star says.

"Thank you girls," I say and hug them.

"That's okay Mummy," Star whispers.

I bite my lip and look to Joseph.

"The girls wanted to know if they can call you Mummy," Joseph says.

I look to Ivy and Nick I don't want to disrespect anyone but they nod and we all hug.

"Of course it's okay," I say. "I love both of you."

Joseph comes over with his present.

"Daddy has something special for you too," Star says.

"Girls, can you help?" Joseph says.

They start singing 'We Wish You A Merry Christmas' and I giggle.

"Holly it's been a crazy few weeks and this may be too soon but who cares? My life has been so dark and sad and then you came in and made me happy, you made the girls happy as well," Joseph says.

"Daddy, just get on with it," Seren says and rolls her eyes. Joseph gets down on one knee.

"Will you marry me?" he asks and I open the box he hands me. A beautiful ring is sitting in the velvet side of the box. It's absolutely stunning and I can't believe it's for me.

"You're supposed to say yes," Star whispers to me and I cry and laugh.

"Yes," I say and slip it on. The girls hug me and Joseph joins in. Nick and Ivy also join in and I can't believe I have the most perfect family in the world. Life can be amazing when it throws you a curve ball but sometimes you just have to be crazy and take that car route you've never done before. It might lead to the perfect life you've always dreamt of.

The End

THANK YOU

Thank you so much for taking the time to read my new book. I hope you have enjoyed it. If you would take a few moments, I would really appreciate it if you left me a review.

Amazon

Goodreads

TRADEMARK ACKNOWLEDGEMENT

A Village Called Christmas features the following trademarked items... The author acknowledges the trademarked status and trademarks owners of the following wordmarks mentioned in this work of fiction.

Musicians and songs

- Kenny Rogers
- Dolly Parton
- Mariah Carey
- Wham
- Nat King Cole
- George Michael
- Wham. "Last Christmas." Music From The Edge Of Heaven, Columbia. 1984. CD
- McCartney, Paul. 'Wonderful Christmastime.' McCartney II. *Parlophone Columbia*. 1979. CD
- Carey, Mariah. 'All I Want For Christmas Is You.' Merry Christmas. *Columbia.*1994. CD
- Buble, Michael 'Santa Claus is Coming to

Town' Christmas. *Reprise 2011*.CD

- Cole, Nat King 'The Christmas Song' The Christmas Song. *Capitol*, 1946. CD
- Menzel, Idinaa 'Let it Go' Frozen: Original Motion Picture Soundtrack. *Walt Disney*. 2013. CD
- Jones, Tom 'Baby it's Cold Outside' Reload. *Gut/V2*. 1999. CD
- Boswell, Eric 'Little Donkey' 1959. Sheet Music
- Jackson five 'Rudolph The Red Nosed Reindeer' Jackson five Christmas album. *Motown*. 1970. CD
- Billy Cotton and His Band featuring Billy Cotton and The Bandits.1953. CD
- Rogers, Kenny & Parton, Dolly 'Islands in the Stream' Eyes That See In The Dark. *RCA Nashville*. 1983. CD

Companies mentioned

- Bucks Fizz
- R&A Bailey & Co
- Mattel, Inc
- Kellogg Company
- Peek Freans
- Nestlé
- Google LLC
- The Walt Disney Company

Films and tv

- Nottinghill. Dir. Roger Mitchell. Julia Roberts, Hugh Grant. Universal Pictures. 1999. Picture
- Frozen. Dir. Chris Buck. Kristen Bell, Idina Menzel. Walt Disney Pictures. 2013. Picture.
- Richard Curtis &Paul Mayhew-Archer (writers) (1994) The Vicar Of Dibley (television) Oxfordshire. Tiger Aspect Productions.
- Splash. Dir. Ron Howard. Tom Hanks, Daryl Hannah, John Candy. Touchstone Films. 1984. Picture.
- Tangled. Dir Nathan Greno & Byron Howard. Walt Disney studio motion pictures. 2010. Pictures.
- Encanto. Dir Bryon Howard. Walt Disney Studio Motion Pictures. 2021. Pictures.

People mentioned
- Kate Winslet
- Tom Hanks
- Sherlock
- Spiderman
- Grinch
- Cinderella

ABOUT THE AUTHOR

Jodie Homer

Jodie lives in a small village in Solihull with her husband and two children. She loves nothing more than dancing around embarrassingly to 90s music and eating mint chocolate. Jodie enjoys reading and writing books full of romance and swoon-worthy fictional men.

SOCIAL MEDIA

To keep up to date with any news on my books or when I will be announcing my next book check out my social media.

Twitter; @jodiehomer11

Instagram; Jodie_loves_books

Goodreads; Jodie Homer

Tiktok @jodiehomerauthor

Threads Jodie Homer

MEET YOU IN THE SUMMER

Chapter 1

December 21st 2017

Lucy

I hate Christmas shopping. Don't get me wrong I love Christmas but the shopping is such a fuss. What do I buy for everyone? And is a gift voucher really that bad? It's so much easier than an actual gift.

I sigh turning the corner of the little alley that leads into the main town centre. There is a beautiful coffee shop that smells of coffee beans. A real rustic style-coffee shop that could easily rival the big guns. The alley is one of my favourite places in the world. It's just a row of little shops all owned by independent businesses.

I step inside 'Coffee to Go' and the bell tinkles. I'm so grateful to stop with all the bags I'm carrying. They've twisted around my hands leaving them red. I shoved them and my coat down at one of the wooden tables with little red napkins on them and walk to the counter.

A man is in front of me with his back to me. He has

broad shoulders in his loose fitted brown jacket. He turns around quickly and everything happens so quickly yet so slowly at the same time. It's exactly like the start of NottingHill.

Coffee goes flying and I feel the wetness and hotness of whatever drink he has ordered. I looked at the barista who looks horrified along with the man who is now holding a tray swamped with his drink.

"Shit, I am so sorry," he says putting the tray down on the table that has my coat and bag on it and handing me tissues he has got out of his pocket. His accent is very noticeably Scottish and I wonder whereabouts he is from.

I use a napkin from my table and dab unsuccessfully at the huge patch on my light blue button up shirt.

"It's okay," I say with a groan, not at all happy.

"Drinks are on me?" he says. I open my mouth to protest and accidentally look into his deep brown eyes.

Well, there are definitely worse-looking men that can spill their drinks all over you.

"Okay," I say and sit down with my bags and coat. Minutes later he brings over a tray of drinks after I tell him what I want.

"I usually don't spill drinks over the prettiest girl in the room," he says and smacks his hand to his head. "I didn't mean that to sound creepy."

I can't help but giggle.

"It's okay," I reassure him. I join in with the red face

and we sit in silence for a second.

"I can be ridiculously clumsy," he admits.

He is pretty lovely to look at. I don't mean to look into his eyes but they aren't just a deep brown they have a tinge of green to them that makes them look mysterious. His hair flops across his face and I wonder how soft it is. Totally inappropriate of course. This would be something my soppy sister would be thinking.

"So, where are you from?" I ask. remembering his lovely accent. No wonder Emilia decided to move there.

"I'm from the Isle of Skye," he says.

"My sister has just moved there. I am heading there tomorrow," I say.

His beautiful jewel-like eyes sparkle and I wonder if this is it. Will I finally find someone who likes me?

"No way, I will be heading back there tomorrow too. Maybe I'll see you on the way." He smiles.

We silently sip our drinks and if I'm honest I would rather be in the car with him a complete stranger than my mum, dad and brother.

"Maybe you will," I say with a smile.

"I would love to take you for a better drink that I won't throw all over you," he says.

I look down at my top that is now stained. Probably one for the bin but I don't think I will ever throw it away.

"It's okay," I reassure him again.

"So, you've been shopping?" he asks, making conversation.

"The joys of Christmas shopping, I have to get it all now so I can pack it away for our holiday." I roll my eyes.

"Do you not like Christmas?" he asks. His eyes twinkle in the light and my stomach jolts like it's been electrocuted.

"Of course I do," I say enthusiastically. "I hate the shopping part."

"Phew," he says pretending to wipe his brow. "I mean, not like that's a deal breaker, but if you didn't like Christmas I wouldn't be able to sit with you through association. In case I was banished and disgraced."

I giggle again.

"It's a good job I do then," I say.

"For sure." He nods.

"What are you doing after you've been here?" I ask. Am I fishing for a date? I'm not even sure anymore but I feel giddy.

"I am done working for the day so I was going to head home," he says.

"What do you do then?" I ask.

"I'm a fisherman," he says.

I must be gawping at him.

"Is that really that unbelievable. Do you want to smell my van?" he asks.

I laugh. "Is that your pick up line?"

"No, oh god it sounds cheesy doesn't it?" he says. I see his cheeks redden.

"More fishy than cheesy," I say back.

We erupt in fits of giggles and I feel our legs brush. I can't help liking the sensation.

"So do you have to leave straight away?" he asks when we stop laughing.

"No, not straight away. Why, are you asking me on a date?" I ask. The glow on his cheeks makes me smile. He's adorable.

"I might be," he says.

We down the last of our drinks and gather up our things.

"I might say yes," I say. He even helps me with my bags as we walk out onto the freezing cold cobble street towards the shops. By now they are mostly closing as the sky is slowly darkening.

"Excuse my manners. I never asked what you do for a living," he asks.

"I work in an office and yes, it's as boring as it sounds," I say.

"Sorry I couldn't hear you over my yawning," he says putting his hand over his mouth.

"I am severely hungover today after the office party last night and I have to spend most of tomorrow in the car with my annoying little brother," I say.

"Well I'm pleased you stopped here for a coffee before your expedition," he says.

"Me too," I say.

We stop underneath the clock tower that towers that seems to reach all the way into the sky that is filling slowly with stars. It doesn't feel like I was at the coffee shop with Maxwell for long at all.

"I have an idea," he says. His eyes are twinkling and I wonder what I am going to get myself into.

"I am not stealing anything," I warn him. He chuckles.

"Trust me," he says and holds out his arm like he is Aladdin. I take his hand feeling safe with him. He instantly makes me feel like mashed potato.

We walk a short distance more and he loosely has his hands over my eyes. This is the weirdest and best date I've ever been on. Is it a date? Am I reading the signs wrong?

"Ta-da," he says uncovering my eyes.

I look around curiously and see that we are standing in what is usually the village green but currently it has a huge ice rink with squealing children and couples skating around.

"After spilling coffee on me, are you sure this is a good idea?" I ask.

"I am deeply offended," he says with a grin.

"I haven't been ice skating since I was little," I say excitedly.

Our hands linger closely as we walk to get our shoes. When we have tied them I link my arm through his and head onto the ice.

"If I go down you know you will too," he says.

"Oh no, I will let go of you and then laugh," I say.

We slowly skate in a circle and actually we aren't too bad. He has wobbled a couple of times but I take his hand and its firm in mine.

"Do you do this every year?" I ask as we rest against the banners.

"What, bump into a pretty girl and take them ice skating? Yes, it is my signature move." He smiles at me and I laugh.

"Well, aren't I the lucky one this year," I say.

He squeezes my hand and I feel a rush of energy surge through me.

We turn to each other on the ice and I feel the world stop. I catch my breath and breathe in the cold air. It's mad that I don't even know his last name but I want to kiss him more than anything. Our cold noses touch first and then our lips find each other. I think this might be the best kiss of my life and my heart definitely agrees.

"Do you believe in fate?" I ask when we pull away. I feel fireworks inside me.

"I never did. A load of old tosh," he says.

"I have an idea," I say and I see his eyes light up. What is he thinking I'm going to say?

"Why don't we not swap numbers?" I say.

"Was my kissing that bad?" he asks and I pretend to hit him. We slide off of the ice and sit down under the towns Christmas tree.

"No," I say. I link my arm through his and smiles up at him.

"You don't believe in fate so why don't we test it?

What do we have to lose?" I ask. This might be the most bat shit thing I've ever thought of.

"Okay." He nods slowly.

"And then, if life doesn't get in the way and we both meet here, we know it's fate. And if it does... well, this has been fun," I say.

Printed in Great Britain
by Amazon

45825964R00138